THE VISIONARY PAGEANT

NewCon Press Novellas

Set 1: Science Fiction (Cover art by Chris Moore)
The Iron Tactician – Alastair Reynolds
At the Speed of Light – Simon Morden
The Enclave – Anne Charnock
The Memoirist – Neil Williamson

Set 2: Dark Thrillers (Cover art by Vincent Sammy)
Sherlock Holmes: Case of the Bedevilled Poet – Simon Clark
Cottingley – Alison Littlewood
The Body in the Woods – Sarah Lotz
The Wind – Jay Caselberg

Set 3: The Martian Quartet (Cover art by Jim Burns)
The Martian Job – Jaine Fenn
Sherlock Holmes: The Martian Simulacra – Eric Brown
Phosphorous: A Winterstrike Story – Liz Williams
The Greatest Story Ever Told – Una McCormack

Set 4: Strange Tales (Cover art by Ben Baldwin)
Ghost Frequencies – Gary Gibson
The Lake Boy – Adam Roberts
Matryoshka – Ricardo Pinto
The Land of Somewhere Safe – Hal Duncan

Set 5: The Alien Among Us (Cover art by Peter Hollinghurst)
Nomads – Dave Hutchinson
Morpho – Philip Palmer
The Man Who Would be Kling – Adam Roberts
Macsen Against the Jugger – Simon Morden

Set 6: Blood and Blade (Cover art by Duncan Kay)
The Bone Shaker – Edward Cox
A Hazardous Engagement – Gaie Sebold
Serpent Rose – Kari Sperring
Chivalry – Gavin Smith

Set 7: Robot Dreams (Cover art by Fangorn)
According To Kovac – Andrew Bannister
Deep Learning – Ren Warom
Paper Hearts – Justina Robson
The Beasts Of Lake Oph – Tom Toner

THE VISIONARY PAGEANT

ARRAYED BEFORE HER

Paul Di Filippo

NEWCON
PRESS

NewCon Press
England

First published in the UK by NewCon Press
41 Wheatsheaf Road, Alconbury Weston, Cambs, PE28 4LF
September 2022

NCP291 (limited edition hardback)
NCP292 (softback)

10 9 8 7 6 5 4 3 2 1

ISBN:

978-1-914953-36-1 (hardback)
978-1-914953-37-8 (softback)

Cover art and front cover graphics by Justin Tan
Back cover layout by Ian Whates

Editorial meddling by Ian Whates
Typesetting by Ian Whates

ONE
SOPHRONIA TEMPEST BEGINS HER DAY

That there should defiantly remain, in this day and age of vast scientific revelations and accomplishments, any perplexing happenings – especially instances of phenomena tinged with the occult – was to the mind of Sophronia Tempest both a philosophical affront and a personal challenge. She regarded any notionally inexplicable doings or enigmatic incidents as blots upon her portrait of reality, a challenging, insolent glove slapped, so to speak, across the face of the human intellect.

After all, was not this year of 1886 a time of perfected marvels derived from science, concrete proof of the power of natural philosophy? Ten mighty arc lights blazed nightly in Market Square, with their power supplied from the newly launched Rhode Island Electric Lighting Company. Many homes were looking forward to that glorious day, supposedly in the next year or three, when they could acquire and install in their parlour the perfected version of one of Thomas Edison's marvellous phonographs, along with a supply of wax cylinder recordings, perhaps featuring renditions even of such popular tunes as "Two Lovely Black Eyes, Oh, What a Surprise" and "Somebody's

Mother." In Germany, a fellow named Karl Benz had leaped the practical hurdles to the creation of an internal combustion engine, powered by the miracle fuel of gasoline. And as far back as 1877, had not the future-minded citizenry of Rhode Island played host to President Rutherford B. Hayes, who had placed the first presidential telephone call? He spoke over a line that connected the Rocky Point Amusement Park with the City Hotel in Providence, all of fourteen miles apart! Such an instrument must soon grace every household of even moderate means.

Yes, these glittering tokens and many more marked this era as the apex of humankind's inventive prowess. Of this, Sophronia Tempest was sure.

Although only twenty years old, Sophronia was a young woman who held and frequently manifested, to the chagrin and ire of many of her unenlightened elders and her male peers, very firm beliefs and opinions about nature and the world, including the sciences and their handmaiden, technology. The reasonableness and susceptibility to understanding that God's creation exhibited was the foundation of her view of existence. She had been inculcated with this attitude at St. Mary's Seminary, that novel and progressive school located in the sprawling and repurposed Howard Mansion in Riverside, a community across Narragansett Bay from Sophronia's home in Providence, Rhode Island.

The boarding school for girls aged five through eighteen had opened in 1874, just in time to receive the eight-year-old Sophronia Tempest. The subsequent ten years there, under the broad-minded and surprisingly liberal aegis of director Sister Mary Juliana Purcell, had infused the growing girl with a love of natural philosophy, reinforcing her natal disposition towards inquisitiveness. Her holidays and summers spent away from the precincts of St. Mary's were idylls of further self-directed reading and backyard experiments.

Her father, Clarence Tempest, a vice-president at Kendall Manufacturing Company, purveyors of the marvellous Soapine ('Soapine, the Dirt Killer! It Washes Everything!' [This motto appended to an illustration of a child scrubbing a dirty whale.]), and her mother, Minnie, happily indulged their daughter's proclivities and interests, although there had been occasional disasters and rebukes, such as the time when she was discovered in the process of sending her infant brother Oscar aloft in a basket tethered to a homemade hot-air balloon. ("But I just wanted to see how high he could go before his breathing became laboured! I would have hauled him right down!")

Having graduated with honours from Saint Mary's, but with no clear vision of how best to pursue her various interests, Sophronia had embarked on a further regimen of studies at the Rhode Island Normal School, with the goal of becoming a teacher. But three semesters at the college had dissuaded her from that career. She found, in a mandated field trial among actual children, that attempting to impart her sophisticated knowledge and enthusiasm to a room full of uninterested brats was highly boring and unsatisfying. Having left the Normal School, Sophronia was at loose ends for only a few weeks, until a revelation struck her.

Although formal teaching did not appeal, and the actual practice of science seemed foreclosed to her and her sex – unless she were prepared to forsake all else in her life and endure a steady stream of contumely and harassment (despite the success of a few rare exemplary foremothers whom she revered, such as the astronomer Maria Mitchell and the botanist Jane Colden) – there remained one route to staying abreast of current developments in the sciences and even contributing in her own way to their dissemination and furtherance. And that method was the practice of journalism.

As a newspaper scribe, Sophronia believed, she would have access to the laboratories and congresses of researchers, and to the factory floors of those titans of industry such as Edison and Westinghouse. She would be able to continue her own education and appreciation of the sciences, while simultaneously enlightening the public, serving as a handmaiden to progress.

And so Sophronia – with some admitted help from her father, who was after all responsible for the placement of a rather large number of weekly advertisements for Soapine in various publications – managed to secure a position at the state's largest newspaper, the *Manufacturers & Farmers Journal* – the *Journal*, for short. A couple of months ago, Sophronia had joined the ranks of the *Journal*'s apprentice reporters.

But, alas, her career had not proceeded exactly as she had dreamed. Very frustrating.

This misdirection or under-utilisation of her talents was the very matter she intended to take up with her superior, Mack Callender, today.

But at the kitchen breakfast table on that morning of June 3, 1886, Sophronia made no mention of any vocational controversies, not wishing to hear another lecture from her father about gratitude and humility, nor endure her mother's advice about the virtues of patience. Instead, she broached an innocent topic in which she actually had some mild interest. As Clarence Tempest unconsciously stroked his luxuriant tawny moustaches while studying the latest number of *Hygeia: the Soap Industry Weekly*; and eternally placid Minnie Tempest improved the unforgiving minute with some sock-darning; and twelve-year-old

4

Oscar Tempest, a veritable freckled demon in short pants, wrestled with Clutterbuck the ginger tomcat, she asked, "Has anyone heard whether or not the Mayor is expected to be well enough to march in the anniversary celebrations?"

This very year marked the two-hundred-and-fiftieth anniversary of the founding of Providence by Roger Williams in 1636. Exile from censorious Massachusetts in search of 'soul liberty', the bold explorer had arrived in that long-ago year at the head of Narragansett Bay, to greet the baffled yet friendly natives with the now-famous hail of 'What cheer, Netop?'. Williams had laid the foundation for all the subsequent glory that was to follow. Nowadays, Providence, second only in the New England region to Boston, was a small dynamic metropolis and an industrial and trade powerhouse, her ships sailing to the Far East and into whaling waters, as well as to Europe and other familiar precincts.

Naturally enough, such a proud and shining city desired and deserved a large and splendid commemoration of such a milestone anniversary, and elaborate plans had been underway for an entire year. The anticipated speeches, parades, cotillions, fireworks, competitions, banquets, picnics, concerts and awards ceremonies would fully occupy the city – and the entire state – for two whole days, June twenty-third and twenty-fourth.

And no one had been more of a champion and inspiration for the whole shebang than Mayor Thomas Doyle, a selfless fellow of vast intellect, virtue and probity. In office on and off for nearly eighteen years, his name was practically synonymous with the city and its reputation. If anyone deserved to bask in the glow of the festivities, to accept the accolades of the populace, it was he. But, alas, Doyle's health had been faltering of late, and his condition was on everyone's mind and lips.

5

Putting aside his journal, Clarence Tempest said thoughtfully, "I had lunch yesterday at the Hope Club, and old Blodget said he heard directly from Doyle's physician that the man had the constitution of an ox and would soon rebound from any temporary incapacity. I would not count him out just yet."

Now came an interruption from the region of the massive coal-fired Smith & Anthony Hub Range.

"Clear the decks! Johnnycakes for all!"

There stood young Bertha Ahlquist, maid and cook to the Tempest household. The plump and jovial seventh daughter of a family of Swedish immigrants resident in the large Scandinavian community in the adjacent town of Cranston, Bertha served the household in exemplary fashion, as she now illustrated, approaching the table with heavy skillet held effortlessly aloft. She efficiently served the steaming cornmeal cakes, then headed off to the laundry room.

Minnie Tempest picked up the thread of her husband's observation. "I surely hope the man perks up enough to enjoy all that he's wrought. He certainly deserves the rewards of his labours."

Releasing Clutterbuck, who scrambled out of the kitchen wildly, Oscar sauced his portion with about a pint of maple syrup, speared several sausages from the platter in the middle of the table, and commenced to devour the whole assemblage like a Fijian cannibal tucking into a serving of missionary.

"I heartily approve of Mayor Doyle," Sophronia said. "He wants to electrify the streetcars, and that's progress. I'm going to ask at the *Journal* if they've heard anything about his health."

Having devastated his breakfast, Oscar paused long enough to venture a question. "Say, Pop, how's the float for Soapine coming along? Can I get a look at it yet?"

Part of the anniversary celebrations was to be a giant Trades Procession, in which scores of retailers and wholesalers, manufacturers, importers and farmers; photographers, blacksmiths and a myriad other craftsmen would display their wares and skills, via creative arrangements atop wagons and suchlike vehicles.

Clarence Tempest chuckled. "It's going to be a whizzer, son, I can tell you that. I had not a small hand in its conception and execution myself. But I'm afraid you'll have to wait until the twenty-fourth to see the float in all its glory, just like everyone else."

"Drat! What good is it having a father in high places if his son don't get no preference?"

Practically levitating off his chair and almost halfway across the kitchen, Oscar said, on the run, "Bye now! I'm off to Billy Budlong's house. We're going to go spear frogs down at the Cove!"

The remaining members of the Tempest family finished their breakfast in a quieter and less frenetic manner, and, upon wiping the last of the maple syrup from her lips, Sophronia kissed her parents goodbye and prepared to depart for the *Journal*.

"You'll be home for dinner, Soph dearest, won't you?" asked Minnie.

"Unless Mister Callender assigns me to cover President Cleveland's White House honeymoon!"

In the entryway she paused before a large mirror to check her looks. (The nearby framed Haskell and Allen lithograph of "Winter in the Country" was so familiar as to be invisible.)

A black felt derby with a white band complemented her light hair and fair skin. Her simple red and yellow sateen daydress looked practical yet handsome, and accentuated her fine corseted

7

waist and modest but sufficient bosom. Common-sense cloth-topped high-buttoned shoes with a low heel allowed her excellent pedestrian mobility, a necessity for a reporter on the go. The whole rig had cost her under ten dollars at a sale at Gladding's Department Store, an economy of which she was proud.

Sophronia exited the family home, a modest manse at 380 Broadway, designed and built just two decades ago by architect Perez Mason. The house's unique third-floor dormer, resembling a lady's Easter bonnet, made the home a local landmark. The leafy neighbourhood represented an elite residential part of the city, second in importance only to the East Side, the district that hosted Brown University.

Nodding to several of the many passersby, Sophronia resolved to walk to the *Journal* offices at 29 Weybosset, a pleasant stroll of fifteen minutes or so.

But when she stepped down from the porch, there on the sidewalk she saw written in chalk a sign of the inexplicable matter that had been so affronting her rational sensibilities for the past few weeks.

The legend read:

ALL THE CATS ARE GOING TO ULTHAR

TWO
WHERE IS ULTHAR?

Sophronia could feel her ire rising. Realising that one of her character defects was a tendency to respond instantly, thoughtlessly and passionately to any perceived slight against one of her particular crotchets, she deliberately throttled back her emotions. After all, should Reason not remain enthroned as Queen above the more primitive faculties? Although sometimes people's stupidity, ignorance and stubbornness did infuriate one!

This deliberately enigmatic graffito played upon a very real phenomenon, the issue that had been scandalising Sophronia's sense of cause and effect.

For the past three months, the feline citizens of Providence had been going missing at an alarming rate, much greater than the annual statistical average for disappearing cats. From many a household each morning arose the wails and sobs of children who woke to discover that poor Puss was nowhere to be found.

Now, in a scientific world such an anomalous burst of disappearances could have had any number of causes. A new disease running rampant among the cat population. A rash of cat-nappings by vivisectionists, or perhaps by members of some alien racial grouping that found cats to be fodder rather than pets. An influx of predators, such as wolves. (The image of a big grey timber wolf, long extinct in New England, slinking through the clothesline-decorated backyards of the city made Sophronia smile for a moment.) These causes and others could be logically justified.

However, there was no evidence to support any of these hypotheses. No cat corpses, intact or savaged. No reports of either medical students avaricious for anatomical knowledge or indiscriminate "chop suey" chefs. No unprecedented larcenous depredations from the desperate farmers of Rhode Island who might wish to recruit barn cats to combat some nonexistent tide of crop-nibbling rats.

And yet, cats continued to disappear.

And then, in the wake of this mystery, had come outbreaks of an infuriating slogan, scrawled hither and yon across Providence:

ALL THE CATS ARE GOING TO ULTHAR.

What could it possibly mean? How could dumb animals choose a destination and then decide to flee, en masse? Where was "Ulthar?" Certainly it was no New England place; and, if far removed from Providence, how could a cat travel there? What lure might draw cats to this unmapped region, away from comfortable homes and cosseting humans? No, the graffito was palpably the work of one or more pranksters, a rude jape intended to capitalise cruelly on the loss of beloved pets. And as such, it really 'got up Soph's nose', to put it coarsely in the manner of brother Oscar.

Using the tip of one shoe, Sophronia effaced the chalked motto, and then strode resolutely off, east down Broadway, heading for the centre of the city and the offices of her employer.

Horse-drawn municipal trams paced her down the middle of the road, flanked on either side by rolling delivery wagons and personal conveyances. The smell of horse manure was not unpleasant, although the coming heat of August might evoke a different reaction to the piles.

The gorgeous June weather and her bold ambulation beneath the stately elms that lined the avenue soon caused her cloud of petulance to dissipate. Additionally, Sophronia had conceived of a plan to attack the enigma. First, she would consult various reference works at the office of the *Journal* in an attempt to pin down the meaning of "Ulthar". Should she fail to find an answer on her own, she would next consult Professor Charnley. Surely that savant would have an answer!

Sophronia had made the acquaintance of Professor Aurion Charnley during her enrolment at the Normal School. Although employed as a respected and elderly faculty member in the Ethnology and Anthropology Department at Brown University, the erudite, albeit somewhat scatterbrained and occasionally caustic fellow had deigned to present a course in the pedagogical techniques of other nations to the budding teachers. (The carnal reinforcements to memory utilised by the Dayaks of Borneo had been scandalous but enlightening.) Sophronia had been his star student, and had maintained an on-and-off, improbable relationship with the older man ever since. Realising now that she had not spoken to Charnley in at least six months, Sophronia castigated herself for letting their friendship lapse just because of the demands of her new job. Surely he of anyone, with his wide knowledge of the odder corners of the globe, would be able to pin down this Ulthar! And perhaps fresh knowledge would point towards a culprit in these sidewalk and board-fence defacements. Such a 'scoop', to employ the reporter's lingo, would surely get her gruff and generally implacable boss to look on her more admiringly and to grant her assignments that were more in accordance with her talents and interests.

Broadway descended gradually at a very slight incline, aiming for the sea-level elevation of the city's downtown. Once on the outskirts of that district, Sophronia zagged a few blocks south to pick up Weybossett, then turned east again. At number 89, she paused outside the Theatre Comique to admire the poster for their latest show: *Pepita; or, the Girl with the Glass Eyes*. Then, continuing onward, just a few doors down from the antique Arcade, an enclosed pavilion of small shops, she found the entrance to the *Journal* offices beckoning.

Inside, the cramped headquarters was a hurly-burly of noisy activity, as reporters, editors, stenographers, pressmen, copyboys, sketch artists and engravers came and went about their duties. (There was talk of hiring a photographer soon, in light of the accomplishments at the *New York Daily Graphic*, where successful reproduction of photographs was now a daily matter.) A small corps of 'newsies', the raggedy, motley youths who delivered the papers to homes, hung about, although their pickup times occurred much later in the day. Most were orphans, simply hoping to cadge a meal.

Largest contributor to the aural chaos were the active ranks of Sholes and Glidden Type-Writers, those marvellous instruments newly perfected and marketed by the Remnigton Sewing Machine Company.

Sophronia wended her way through the scrum. At one desk, she paused.

There sat her rival. At least she conceived of the fellow as such, although he probably did not regard her in the same light. But he was the reporter who most often secured the plum assignments from editor Mack Callender, the kind of stories that Sophronia dreamed of writing. And, gallingly, he was not much older than she.

Clean-shaven and ruggedly handsome, often to be discovered with an insouciant smile playing about his lips, Reuben Standeven wore a nicely tailored sack suit with houndstooth vest, a colourful foulard around his throat. Engaged in earnestly studying some papers, he idly skritched his scalp through wavy auburn hair.

Sensing Sophronia's presence, he looked up and brightened.

"What cheer, fair damsel! May I say you look most beguiling this morning? Fit to consort with the grand dames at the Art Club – but in the role of ingenue only."

Sophronia snorted. "Such is not my aim. What are you perusing there?"

"Information on the latest Corliss steam engine. I am to interview the great George Corliss himself this afternoon."

Sophronia found herself deprived of the powers of speech. This was exactly the kind of hard-edged reportorial task she herself coveted! And for which she was perfectly adapted! And yet, despite all her begging and imploring, she was relegated to covering teas and soirees, theatrical performances, school fairs, quilting bees and similar dainty and 'feminine' activities.

Sophronia knew that Reuben was not bragging, nor rubbing this peach assignment in her face. Nonetheless, she turned without a civil word and huffed off.

She did not look back, because she suspected the infuriating man would be grinning.

Pausing only briefly outside Mack Callender's office door, Sophronia knocked and entered.

The editor's office was decorated with framed lithographs from various magazines, such as *The Judge* and *Puck*. They all flaunted a satirical cast, poking savage fun at mankind's foibles, such as the depiction of a bribe-taking policemen, titled "Hush money – or money for the sewer". Additionally, there were framed copies of front pages to which Callender had contributed.

She found her boss speaking on the telephone. That miraculous device, one of some fifty thousand now extant across the country, intrigued Sophronia no end, and she longed to take the 'gadget' apart to examine its innards.

Spotting Sophronia, the editor waved her to a seat.

"Yes, yes," Callender was expostulating, "I know all that!"

Sophronia used her boss's preoccupied state to marvel anew at his formidable appearance.

Dressed in striped trousers and fawn-coloured cutaway coat, Mack Callender was a bantam of a fellow, but vigorous and hard as nails. Some fifty years old, he possessed a phiz that bore many scars – and only one eye, his vacant orbit being concealed with a piratical patch. Likewise, one empty sleeve of his jacket was pinned up at the shoulder.

Callender had been a veteran reporter for the *Hartford Daily Courant* until two years ago. Covering the Tonkin War between the French and the Chinese, he had been blown up by a mine. After a long recovery, he returned to his post only to find the *Courant* shuttering shop. But he came to regard the closing as fortuitous, since it caused him to realise that his best field days were behind him and that desk work was now his lot. The owners of the *Journal* had snapped him up as an editor as soon as they heard of his availability.

Having been a reporter himself for so long, Callender knew the desires and wiles, the deceits and demands of his staff intimately.

Callender replaced the earpiece of the telephone back on its hook and focused his fierce one-eyed glare on Sophronia like the beam from a powerful lighthouse.

"What do you want? I suppose you've discovered I'm sending Standeven to the Corliss factory instead of you! And why not? The boy is a quick study. He'll do a bang-up interview. And he won't belabor poor Corliss with a thousand dreamy questions about gasket dimensions and pipe-fitting tolerances and the future of 'steam men of the prairies', like someone I could name. Am I correct, or am I not, Miss Tempest?"

Sophronia had to bite her tongue before replying. "Your forceful remarks display your usual vivid candour, Mister Callender."

The editor burst out into hearty laughter. "You don't back down, and you're a diplomat, girl! I predict that if you just restrain your more unnatural predilections, you'll go far in this business."

The compliment fought with her irritation, and achieved an uneasy truce. "Thank you, sir. Might I now enquire what you had on tap for me today? Another strawberry festival perhaps? The Board Meeting at the Providence Athenaeum? Maybe some heiress in Newport has a hangnail?"

Callender harrumphed. "You fail to realise that such homely items draw readers to our pages in possibly even greater numbers than fantastical accounts of some crackpot inventor and his Vernean submersible. And we need readers, so as to stay fiscally afloat. And you have a knack for rendering such quotidian items interesting. However, none of your acidulous darts have quite hit the mark. I want you to attend a lecture tonight. The speaker is a woman named" – Callender rummaged through some memoranda –"named Isadora Blank. Apparently she's been

15

making speeches here in Providence for the past several months, but it's only now that she's come to my attention, as her popularity waxes."

"What is the topic of her lectures?"

"It's some kind of self-help pap. From what I can make out, a blend of Emerson and Fourier, with a soupçon of Samuel Smiles. But in any case, she's beginning to draw crowds, and we need to render an account of her tripe."

Sophronia sighed dramatically. "I will endeavour to transcribe her wisdom accurately and objectively."

Callender's attention was already shifting to other matters. "Good, good, I knew I could count on you. Here's two tickets. Make a night of it. Take that beau of yours. What's his name? Bowtie? Arthur Bowtie?"

"Arthur Botwink," said Sophronia, feeling that familiar sense of damp and tepid amiability arise in her bosom as the image of Arthur swam into her mind's eye.

THREE

LITTLE PITCHERS HAVE BIG EARS

With a tide of noontime pedestrians surging around her – in the street an ice wagon was followed by a bread wagon, which in turn was followed by a butcher's pushcart and a pack of curs – Sophronia stood outside the Hoppin Homestead Building, 287 and 289 Westminster Street, still within the downtown area and just a short walk away from the *Journal* offices. The lavish display windows of the building featured colourful ceramics and pots, dishes and platters, cups and pitchers of every style and size, all tastefully arranged on red satin-draped risers. Here was the prestigious outlet of Warren & Wood Crockery, purveyors to the carriage trade. The establishment that employed her boyfriend, Arthur Botwink, as a staff overseer.

Sophronia ransacked her brain for reasons not to enter.

She had spent a large part of the morning after leaving Callender's office in the *Journal*'s small but mighty reference library, examining the *Encyclopædia Britannica* and many other sources, such as atlases and traveller's accounts, to see if she could ascertain the meaning or location of 'Ulthar'. But her digging had met with no success. Reluctantly abandoning that investigation, she had been given the task of visiting the offices of the Cecilia Society to ascertain when their next chamber music concert would occur, and who the performers would be. Although Sophronia harboured a place for music in her engineer's soul, she found the bustle-wearing, matronly head of the Cecilia Society a complete snooze. She feared she had affronted the woman by letting a tremendous yawn escape during the course of the interview. Oh well, the old harpy should be glad that any attention at all was being paid to her and her boring antique club of dry-as-dust aesthetes.

After returning to the offices and writing up her inconsequential piece – the chafing figure of Reuben Standeven was nowhere to be seen – Sophronia realised it was lunch hour, and time for her daily repast with Arthur Botwink.

And so, here she was. But while most days found her slightly anticipatory of her meeting with Arthur, in the humdrum manner of a child who had been told of the forthcoming visit of a maiden aunt who always dispensed one's least favourite candy, today Sophronia found herself positively reluctant to see her beau.

What could be the matter with her? What imp of the perverse had so unsettled her today, and made her actually resent having to lunch with Arthur?

She had known him since they were both five years old, and they had grown up practically side by side, save when different schools parted them. Their families had been commingled for ages, and somehow it had become a *fait accompli* that she and Arthur were practically destined to be mated someday, like the only two animals of the same species in the zoo. Attending an all-girls school as she had, Sophronia had not been subjected daily to a wide variety of alternative suitors during her tender years. Nor had she really missed or sought out such male company, being preoccupied with her other interests. The adult social occasions she enjoyed these days always seemed to include Arthur at her side, thus warding off any potential rival swains. Sophronia had neither resented nor even meditated on this pre-connubial condition until recently, when she had begun to experience certain fancies regarding her ideal helpmeet and romantic ideal. Nebulous images had of late begun to fill the mirror of her mind, and none of them resembled Arthur in the slightest.

And yet, she could not find it in herself to break off whatever tacit and circumspect – and dull, dull, dull! – lovers' arrangement she and Arthur implicitly shared. The fellow, she was sure, would positively collapse! And certainly he had done nothing ill-mannered or inconsiderate to merit her rebuke.

Thank the Lord that at least there had yet been no talk of setting a date for their marriage!

And so, as conflicted and irresolute as ever – an emotional and mental condition which she experienced in no other area of her life – Sophronia pushed open the doors of Warren & Wood and went in search of her dining partner.

After crossing the busy and elegant sales floor, she found Arthur standing a few steps high on a ladder, and busy overseeing the erection of a display, as two junior shopboys under his direction tried to instantiate his conceptions.

"No, no, we need to see the imagery in a *panoramic* way!"

Arthur Botwink showed a medium height and the physique of some lolling adolescent on a Greek urn (a metaphorical comparison quite in keeping with his chosen trade, thought Soph). His straw-coloured hair was already thinning, but even a thicker thatch would have definitely failed to conceal protuberant ears. Alas, his chin did not possess the most commanding dimensions, being rather underslung. His large blue eyes,

19

although quite charming, did have a tendency to mist over upon any maudlin pretext, such as the coming of autumn or the recitation of "The Song of Hiawatha."

Sophronia made a quick mental comparison of Arthur's looks against that still-somewhat-unformed Adonis growing in her imagination, and sighed.

Spotting his inamorata, Arthur grinned widely, in a rather moony fashion. He climbed down, snagging one of the display items.

"Curtis, Herbert, you are dismissed until after lunch."

The boys eagerly departed.

Arthur cradled the object in his hands in the manner of a rajah holding a jewel of great price. "Look, dear, isn't this simply fabulous?"

Sophronia saw nothing unusual: a white pitcher of classical proportions, with a band of painted daisies around the rim. The belly of the object held a famous scene, rendered in exquisite detail in an umber monotone: Roger Williams standing in the prow of a small boat as it came ashore to the amazement of the local Indians. The date of 1636 showed on a banner below the portentous, city-foundational meeting.

"We commissioned these just for the anniversary celebrations. Mister Warren expects to sell a powerful grist of these." Arthur lowered his voice to a whisper. "Don't tell anyone, but our wagon in the Trades Procession is going to feature a veritable *ziggurat* of Williams pitchers!"

Sophronia made some polite sounds of approbation, and that seemed to be enough to satisfy Arthur's pride in his employer's wares.

"All this decorative work has stimulated my appetite. I'm famished! Let's head out."

Exiting the store, the pair turned their steps in a familiar direction and ended up at Wambley's Chophouse and Seafood Grotto. The spacious, echoing, rambunctious establishment was packed, but after a short wait a table was found for Sophronia and Arthur. Presented with green pasteboard menus as big as desk blotters, the pair made their choices.

Their waiter – a dissolute, middle-aged Bacchus in a dirty apron – having finally arrived, Arthur reeled off a catalogue of viands that no stranger would have associated with a fellow of his moderate size. But Sophronia knew that he could pack away quantities of food a dock worker would have trouble ingesting – and never add weight. This was perhaps Arthur's only trait that she envied.

"I'll have lobster croquettes followed by the green turtle soup, if you please. Then the lamb chops with asparagus tips, and an oyster plant and dandelion salad too. Oh, some succotash on the side. And lastly, a wedge of gorgonzola and a Biscuit Tortoni to finish."

Arthur turned to Sophronia. "And you, my dear?"

She hesitated a moment, busy thinking of how much cooking any bride of Arthur's would have to do. "I'll take the watercress and shrimp salad. And some Champagne Wine jelly for dessert."

The waiter collected the elephant-folio menus and strode off.

Arthur's face expressed worried concern. "Soph, my love, you really should force yourself to enjoy heartier meals. Not to be coarse, but all the experts agree that a woman has to maintain her internal, ah, mechanisms with a regular and copious supply of calories if she ever hopes to fulfil her maternal function."

"I will be sure to stoke those dire engines at the appropriate season. But right now, I'm more interested in an intellectual matter. Look at these tickets I have for Friday night. I'd like you to come."

Sophronia explained her assignment. Arthur cogitated, then said, "I had wanted us to go to the San Souci or Park Gardens on Friday for some fun. I understand there's a new minstrel troupe coming to the San Souci."

Sophronia felt irritation at Arthur's unsophisticated tastes in entertainment, but did not chide him. "I'd like to see them too, Arthur. But this task is essential to my work."

"Oh, well, then," said Arthur magnanimously, "you may count me in."

Their meals came – steaming, fragrant platters and a mingy bowl of greens – and Sophronia found that her not overly delicate consumption of her small portions was nearly outmatched by Arthur's speedy trencherman devastation of his several plates.

After a round of coffee, they left Wambley's for the Cove Promenade.

A finger of Narragansett Bay extended deep into the centre of Providence, terminating in the circular Cove at the foot of Smith Hill. Despite tidal flushing and being also fed by two streams from the north and west (the Woonasquatucket and the Moshassuck), the body of water had become somewhat noisome as Providence's manufactories thrived. There was talk of someday filling it in and reclaiming the space for buildings. But for the present, a graceful railed esplanade followed the perimeter of the Cove and allowed for pleasant recreational sauntering – if the daily waxing and waning odours cooperated.

Sophronia listened patiently as Arthur spoke of retail doings at Warren & Wood Crockery involving people she barely knew.

Every now and then she managed to share some of her own workplace concerns, receiving reassuring platitudes in return.

As they reached the northernmost arc of the walk, Sophronia espied a group of ragamuffin youths ankle deep in the stinky mud beyond the railing, and recognised Oscar among them. The wildly exuberant boys were jabbing at agitated dye-sickly frogs and unseen tannery-crippled fish with improvised wooden spears. She stopped to admonish her brother.

"Oscar! Mama's going to have a fit when she sees how filthy you are!"

"Oh, don't be such a badger, sis! I'll clean up good before I go home. Anyhow, we aren't going to be here much longer, are we, fellas?"

"Why not? Where are you going next?"

"Oh, me and my chums got a line on the place where all the cats is going."

"Ulthar?"

"That's it. I reckon we can track them down and get them all home."

"Oh, don't be ridiculous! There's no such place."

"We'll see," said Oscar. "Just you wait."

FOUR
THE STARRY SODALITY

The next day, June fourth, was the very Friday of Sophronia's assignment, and she had been itching throughout the long morning to get to the self-improvement lecture by the mysterious yet no doubt unrelievedly banal and boring Isadora Blank. Soph counted on hastening through the lecture with jaundiced eye, (however unprofessional that might be), after which she would distil its essence into a witty screed. True, she would much rather have had the chance to attend a speech by William Stanley at Brown University about his new induction coil and the possibilities of alternating current; or been asked to bask at a salon in the presence of Kate Field, the inspirationally famous female correspondent and paragraphist and friend to Mark Twain, but those options were not open to her. And even if her story were relegated to the society column, it still stood a chance of showcasing her prose talents and perhaps convincing Mack Callender to allow her broader scope.

Sophronia spent the morning helping her mother in their kitchen garden. Sophronia had definite thoughts about new and improved scientific methods of cultivation, and lectured her

24

placid and tolerant mother during the entire operation of weeding and hoeing, mulching and harvesting. After that, she went into the *Journal* offices and helped to compile the shipping news column and aided in the composition of advertisements for Burdock's Blood Bitters and Count Rumford's Baking Powder. Of course, lunch with Arthur intervened. Today they ate less formally – albeit, on Arthur's part, with equal copiousness – enjoying liverwurst sandwiches, milk and gooseberry pie from the W. S. Sweet & Sons lunch wagon, so that Arthur could have time to visit a competitor's store and spy on their new line of merchandise for Warren & Wood.

Sophronia returned home in the late afternoon to enjoy an early supper with family before changing her clothing and awaiting escort Arthur's arrival. During the meal, Clarence Tempest reported on the Mayor's health and the progress of the Trades Procession. Minnie Tempest had to gently berate Bertha the cook for letting the brace of canvasback ducks linger in the oven too long, to the point of dryness. Oscar Tempest surreptitiously read a dime novel involving the Old Sleuth, held beneath the table. He wasn't fooling anyone about where his attention was focused, but his parents indulged him. Sophronia considered exposing her brother's infantile and fantastic scheme to discover the fabulous lands of Ulthar – what if such a pursuit involved dangerous or illicit trespasses? – but then thought better of it. There seemed to be little harm in the game. She recalled her own youthful explorations and transgressions and felt Oscar should enjoy the same liberties.

At eight PM on this balmy June night, with crickets chirruping, Arthur arrived, dressed with meticulous care in a tailcoat and top hat. He chatted politely and familiarly with Clarence and Minnie, with no evident urgency to be away, until

Sophronia dragged him off. They caught the horse-drawn tram that would bring them through the centre of downtown before depositing them on the eastern edge of the district, at Market Square.

On the tram, Arthur noticed that Sophronia clutched a small volume in library binding. "What's that, my dear? The latest number of *Godey's Lady's Book*, per chance? Are you assaying the latest fashions for the fall?" Arthur contorted his face in what he obviously assumed to be the coy and sly manner of a roué making an indecent remark. "Or are you intent on building up your trousseau?"

Sophronia opened the book to its title page. "These are some fairly recent proceedings from the Royal Astronomical Society. I brought them along to occupy me if this Blank woman's speech should prove to be too hideously boring. I'm most interested in this report from Albert Michelson. 'Experimental Determination of the Velocity of Light.' Arthur, have you ever considered the vastness of interstellar space, and all the myriad phenomena those reaches contain? As yet, we know only the smallest fraction of what lies beyond our atmosphere. Why, there might even be new planets relatively close by, just out beyond Neptune!"

Arthur scoffed. "Unless such remote venues hold new customers for Warren & Wood's products, I fear I'm not much interested."

Sophronia sighed, and clapped shut her book.

Under its novel electric arc lights, Market Square seemed a veritable fairyland. The civic space, dominated by the eponymous stately building that dated from before the Revolution, hosted many strollers and idlers of both sexes, including a fair number of Bohemians, obviously attracted or supported by the Rhode Island School of Design, which occupied a suite of six rooms in the same Hoppin Homestead Building that housed Warren & Wood Crockery. Not far away reared the lofty steeple of the First Baptist Church. From this spot the land and streets sloped steeply upward to form the East Side of the city, home to many elegant houses and Brown University. Sophronia recalled her plans to visit Professor Aurion Charnley concerning the origins of Ulthar, and resolved to seek that meeting tomorrow or as soon as possible. However, at this moment she would not be ascending College Hill, but remaining at its base.

Sophronia and Arthur set out to walk the few blocks down South Main Street to their destination. South Main ran parallel to that thrust of the finger of ocean water which supplied the Cove, but it was not the street closest to the water's edge. That avenue was South Water Street, a rough district of warehouses and fish-processing plants, chandlers and coal depositories that serviced the many medium-sized ships tied up at the wharves. (Larger vessels docked at India Point, or further down the Bay.) The time-distressed buildings lining South Main Street did not present an unbroken façade, but at almost every juncture offered narrow and dark alleyways between them, connecting to South Water. Despite being only a block long, these shadowy, smelly, slimy cross-passages seemed, to Sophronia's nervous eye, to twist and turn for miles, harbouring unknown and unknowable denizens. She disliked coming here at night. The uneven brick sidewalks seemed to offer pitfalls and snares. Cursing her unwonted timidity, Sophronia clung tightly to Arthur's arm as they walked along. Arthur straightened his back at the implicit compliment to his protective manliness, and cast defiant glances at whatever might lurk beyond the nimbus of the widely spaced gas lights. The foot traffic was sparse, and Sophronia imagined lascars and cutpurses lurking behind every tree trunk.

Eventually, however, they arrived without instance at the corner of Power and South Main, and the building that was to host Isadora Blank's lecture.

The Amateur Dramatic Hall was a somewhat shabby but still impressive edifice. Originally erected in 1833 as a Methodist Church, it had had a chequered career since, even serving for a time as a riding academy. Nowadays it hosted theatrical performances. Some three storeys tall, it presented its windowless but modestly ornamented brick front to South Main, at the far verge of a small plot of grass serving as front lawn, with the body of the structure running uphill along Power Street; so that although the patron would enter through the front door on the lowest level of the building, should he wish to exit from the rear, he would have to ascend to the Hall's second floor to match the rising street.

A steady stream of patrons of all sexes, ages and distinctions was converging on the entrance from every point of the compass, and Sophronia and Arthur joined them. As they drew closer to the braced-open dual doors, Sophronia registered a small signboard:

HEADQUARTERS OF THE STARRY SODALITY
ISADORA BLANK,
HIEROPHANT AND OPENER OF THE WAY
"WELCOME, ALL YE WHO DESIRE CELESTIAL
PERFECTION"

Sophronia wondered aloud. "Has this unknown sect purchased the whole building? How could they have become so well established so quickly?"

Arthur assumed a mercantile and speculative mien. "I wonder if they need ewers or goblets or salvers for their ceremonies. Warren & Wood could cut a good deal for quantities of a gross or more."

Two attendants, youngish clean-shaven men, flanked the doors. There was nothing untoward or off-putting about their appearance, save for the fact that they wore white belted gowns of some heavy rich fabric such as samite, and stood unshod. One of them collected the tickets proffered by Sophronia with a benign nod and the adjuration, "Reach out for the constellations, my friend, and live."

In the theatre proper, facing the stage at the uphill end of the building and looking over the massed heads of a packed house, with sibilant and reverential whispers predominating, Sophronia paused to assess the audience. Arthur perforce halted as well.

The seated viewers seemed regular citizens of every stripe, rock-ribbed Yankees as well as a smattering of Negroes and Orientals and Mediterranean immigrants. Soph wondered what attraction or platform could have united such a wide spectrum of attendees. Were these all seekers after 'celestial perfection'?

A familiar voice resounded from close behind the preoccupied Sophronia, making her jump.

"What's the matter, Miss Scribbler? Is there no ribbon-bedecked reserved booth for the glorious members of the press?"

Sophronia whipped around to confront a grinning Reuben Standeven. A red film of anger seemed suddenly to intervene between them.

'Why, you greedy, immoral cad! Does your professional jealousy know no bounds, that you had to follow me here to undercut my reportage? I suppose you'll rush back to the *Journal* as soon as this circus is over and file your piece before I can file mine. Well, I won't allow it! I'll –"

Reuben held up a monitory hand. "Hold on, hold on just a minute! I'm not here in a working capacity, and I have no intention of belabouring my creative faculties tonight. I've come to this Chautauqua just for amusement. And it's at the behest of this fine lady, she who proposed our evening's entertainment."

Sophronia finally noticed Reuben's comrade with a start.

A blonde woman clad in expensive velvet and lace, her feet nipped in the most fashionable heels, she displayed more intoxicating curves than any seacoast road on the French Riviera. Her heavily painted face seemed an advertisement for acts of a delightfully immoral turpitude that would register no guilt or regrets. She had the temerity to leer boisterously at Sophronia and say, "Pleased to meet you, lamb's lettuce! My name's Fannie Audet. What's your handle?"

Sophronia stuttered out her name, which suddenly seemed utterly alien on her own lips.

"Fannie is a singer at the San Souci Gardens," said Reuben. "You should hear her rendition of 'Plum Pudding'. Go ahead, Fannie, regale them with a verse!"

Oblivious of the dignified circumstances, Fannie Audet commenced loudly to sing.

"Oh! When you hear the 'whoop,' the milkman's on the stoop,
Awaiting with his jingling can.
Oh, never stop to chat about the pussy cat.
Don't let him call you simple Mary Ann;
Now when he drives away, oh, to yourself you say:
'When I get my Sunday out,
I'll meet him in the park a little after dark,

And hook him as I would a little trout!'"

A dead hush had descended in the theatre during Fannie's gay song, as all heads swivelled to face the rear. But then, plainly forgetting the solemnity and reverence of their gathering, the crowd erupted in applause, hoots and catcalls. Beaming, Fannie took several bows.

Utterly mortified, Soph turned to Arthur for moral support, but found him gawping at the dancehall floozy with a fascination he had always hitherto reserved for Meissen, Delft and Wedgewood handicrafts.

Soph returned her basilisk stare to her coworker. "Mister Standeven, we will have much to thrash out at the office on Monday. But now I have to perform my duties as a reporter."

Sophronia dragged Arthur away to the nearest two empty seats, as Reuben and Fannie found their own places.

"I must say," Arthur averred, "that I don't much care for your snippy fellow reporter. He's overly blithe."

Feeling oddly defensive about Reuben Standeven, Sophronia was going to reply that this was a flaw Arthur would never embody. But she squashed her comment, for now the curtain concealing the stage was beginning to rise.

FIVE

SHE WHO MUST OPEN THE WAY

If Sophronia had anticipated any aspect of tonight's presentation, it had been through fostering vague notions of a lectern on a bare platform, sentried by a spinsterish or schoolmistressly prune of a scold, who would dispense uplifting platitudes and bromides. Or, perhaps, the speaker would be some female avatar of Dr. Kellogg from the Battle Creek Sanitarium, a stern physician-type clad in Hippocratic regalia and advocating exercises with Indian clubs and jump ropes. But neither of these two conceptions could have been further from the actuality of what greeted Sophronia now.

First off, the stage was backdropped by a gaudy stellar panorama painted on canvas. Fiery comets, ringed planets, blazing stars, all cascading in a Newtonianly impossible yet impressive jumble. The next aspect that betrayed Sophronia's prejudices was a divan set centre-stage and surrounded by banks of flowers whose mingled fragrances now disseminated through the hall.

Lastly, and most disturbingly, was the speaker herself.

From the left side of the stage, a magnificent, ageless woman strode forth like Boadicea marching to meet the Roman legions.

Masses of Titian hair framed a classically beautiful face: noble brow, strong cheekbones, perfect mouth, dark eyes. The woman's ample charms were shockingly revealed by a clinging ivory gown of diaphanous material, unlike the stiff brocades worn by her male acolytes at the door. Her waist was limned by a gold belt in the form of a double-headed snake, while delicate sandals clasped her small but strong feet. Overall, she radiated a kind of supreme celestial confidence and power.

Reaching the divan, she turned to face the crowd. Her bare shapely arms remained comfortably by her sides. She did not smile to ingratiate herself, as any other lecturer might have done. Nonetheless her solemn yet supernal visage seemed to beam a warm and nigh-tangible message of embrace to her viewers, a loving sympathy. When she spoke, the tone and timbre of her deep and dulcet voice reeked of pure enchantment.

"Welcome, fellow voyagers among the constellations. My name is Isadora Blank, Hierophant of the Starry Sodality, and I am here tonight to guide you all to the land of your fondest dreams, a realm of languor and plenty. But before we can begin to make ourselves ready to set sail for the Elysian pastures of eternity, a demanding process, we must make a tally of what we willingly leave behind.

"We leave behind all the ills that flesh is heir to.

"We leave behind all the disappointments of our friendships and loves.

"We leave behind all the necessity of earning our bread by the sweat of our brows.

"We leave behind all duties to Caesar, and all dictates of tyranny.

"We leave behind all our gold and treasures.

33

"We leave behind all our worries, fears and doubts, our grief and remorse.

"And what do we gain in return?"

Here Isadora Blank lifted her arms in a wide gesture that invited everyone to shelter in the harbour of her expansive and poorly concealed bosom.

"We gain peace and tranquillity, ease and vigour, joy and zest, in a landscape of purest bliss, that Ultima Thule for which your soul has been ceaselessly questing since before you were born. And that is what I hope to show you now, if the Elder Gods of the Farthest Depths of Space are willing to use me as their conduit."

Despite its lack of flowery oratory – she was no John Bartholomew Gough – Isadora Blank's speech had left her audience mesmerised, their attention rapt. Even Sophronia, armed with her journalistic objectivity, her scientific precepts and her frothy, mild cynicism, felt herself struggling to remain aloof from the beguiling seduction. Looking about, she saw every face displaying pure yearning acceptance, every set of shoulders and every torso straining unconsciously towards the stage, lifting haunches half off their seats. Beside her, Arthur resembled Actaeon halfway through his transformation by Artemis into a stag, his face all mawkish.

Sophronia's gaze happened to light upon the back of Reuben Standeven's head. As if receiving a mental message, her colleague turned to regard her, and transmitted a sly wink, with all his usual irreverence. Apparently he too had not succumbed completely to the allure of Isadora Blank. Somehow this circumstance reassured Sophronia, even though she certainly retained her high dudgeon against the man.

Now Isadora Blank slowly and gracefully lowered her perfect form to the divan, first sitting upon it, then reclining fully and crossing her ankles. Her supine position seemed to release some of the tension in the audience, which let out a collective sigh and settled down in their own seats.

Acolytes lowered the gas lights to the level of an aureate dusk. The crowd seemed to hold its breath.

Above Isadora Blank, a cloudy phosphorescent nebula with irregular borders began to take form. The hazy luminescent mass expanded to engulf the Hierophant and her couch and to fill the centre volume of the stage.

Then, images began to flow across the cloud!

The successive static scenes, colourful as real life, depicted humans, nude save for tastefully placed ribbons and scarves, gambolling or lolling in alien climes, amidst fantastic foliage or in cyclopean plazas, illuminated by foreign spectra. Strange shadowy non-human beings, possessed of many queer limbs and appurtenances, were shown in several scenes, consorting with the humans in several manners subject to various interpretations.

Faster and faster the images succeeded each other across the cloud, a dizzying accelerating parade, a visionary pageant that left subliminal sensory impressions of indescribable and unspeakable vistas, ripe with ineffable meaning.

Just when Sophronia felt herself upon the verge of being overwhelmed, perhaps even of swooning, Isadora rocketed to her feet in a catlike leap, coming to a standing position atop the divan and shattering the cloud into evanescent zooming particles. The audience responded with a cataleptic jolt.

The Opener of the Way thrust her arms skyward and intoned a litany of harsh syllables which Sophronia could only register in part. The next day, attempting to render the words into print, she derived from memory phrases with these semblances:

"Ia, ia! Vulgtm hai vulgtlagln! Ilyaa uh'e wgah'n nglui ch'hupadgh! Azathoth nafln'ghft ftaghu n'ghft syha'h gotha!"

Having completed her forceful arcane invocation, Isadora Blank stepped calmly down off the couch. "Reach out for the constellations, my friends, and live," she said, then walked slowly offstage.

No applause followed her stately exit. The assembled auditors remained transfixed and mute for a full sixty seconds, before finally bursting out into a bedlam of comments and exclamations.

Feeling curiously enervated and drained, yet infused with a kind of eerie galvanic ichor, Sophronia got to her feet. Arthur remained seated, as if dazed, until Sophronia yanked him up. They inched their way with the shuffling crowd into the main aisle and headed toward the front entrance.

At the doors, the acolytes were pressing copies of a single-sheet broadside upon each person. Sophronia took one.

COME CLOSEST
TO THE NUMINOUS SIDEREAL REALM
WHILST YET HERE ON EARTH
BY PAYING A VISIT TO
THE COMMUNE OF
"THE BLACK GOAT OF THE WOODS
WITH A THOUSAND YOUNG"
CHOPMIST HILL
(PERMANENT DWELLERS WELCOMED)

Beneath this invitation was a drawing of a festive pastoral scene straight from the work of Pieter Bruegel, with the addition of a ghostly goat's head floating in the sky over the jolly celebrants, leering down beneficently.

Emerging into the clarifyingly crisp June night air, and halting on the grass aside from the flow of congregants, Sophronia felt her normal disposition and faculties return to her. She could analyse and better take stock of what she had just experienced. Whatever Isadora Blank was selling or preaching, the woman was no ordinary carnival barker or shill. She manifested great charisma and spellbinding potency, akin to that of a Charles Taze Russell or Henry Ward Beecher. But to what end? Surely all that talk of transaetheric migration to other spheres was just a façade for some other goal or activity? But what? There had to be some element of profit involved for the Starry Sodality. But on the basis of what venture? No one tonight had even asked for donations! Perhaps the Commune advertised on the broadside represented the financial end of the operation. Could the Sodality perhaps be drafting gullible folks into working for free, in the fields or in hypothetical manufactories at Chopmist Hill? That seemed almost too tepid and mundane a scheme for such an exotic pitch.

Whatever the rationale or hidden aspects of the Starry Sodality, Sophronia sensed that here was a much larger story than her editor had presumed. Her reporter's nose quivered with anticipation. She resolved to follow this mystery to its ultimate end.

Her whirling thoughts were suddenly halted by a confident proclamation from behind her.

"A magic lantern! That's what it had to be, plain as day. What do you think?"

Reuben Standeven, an arm insouciantly around the slim waist of Miss Fannie Audet, awaited a reaction from Sophronia, to whom he had plainly directed his query. Sophronia could feel Arthur bristling beside her, irked at Reuben's effrontery. But to her bemusement, Sophronia herself was not as put out as she might have been, since Reuben's suggestion appealed to her, and sparked off her own speculations.

"Yes!" she responded excitedly. "Mounted under the divan, perhaps, and projecting its apparitions upward through a series of mirrors. With concealed controls!"

"But what do we make of the gassy substance on which the slides cavorted, in lieu of a more conventional screen? Some kind of muslin or cheesecloth, shredded and blown apart by fans for the finale?"

"If only we could get onto that stage to search for clues!"

But already the doors to the theatre had been shut and locked.

"Might I suggest," said Reuben, "An approach from the rear?"

"I'm game!"

Arthur shuffled backwards in shock. "Sophronia Tempest! You're not planning to sneak into that building, are you? That's highly disrespectful of the organisation and the seeress that just sought to enlighten us."

"Oh, Arthur, you're not telling me you bought that bushel of codswallop Miss Chiffon Loins was selling!"

"I certainly found many aspects of her lecture enticing and provocative of thought. Who would not want to desert this vale of tears for a better home among the heavens? Life is not all crockery and cravats, you know."

Sophronia was astonished. Here was a side of Arthur she had never witnessed till now. But before she could remonstrate with him, Fannie Audet chimed in.

"I'm with this boy! That gal's a pip, a real queen! A royal Cleopatra type. She knows something we don't, and she showed us just the merest glimmering of her wisdom tonight. I know that if I didn't have to sing for my supper every night and let mashers grab at my quim, I'd be a whale happier than I am now."

Sophronia expected Arthur to express horror at Fannie's use of such a vulgar expression. But instead, he moved closer to the singer and said, "Miss Audet, I am fascinated to hear your reaction to Miss Blank's performance, which tallies with mine. It seems that we might derive additional insights by discussing our shared experience."

Reuben let go of Fannie's waist and practically thrust her upon Arthur. "It's settled then! Soph and I will endeavour to learn more here at the theatre, while you two will have a fine confab on mystical matters at Whateley's Coffee House."

Fannie smiled at Arthur, giving the impression somehow of a peckish lioness. "I ain't disinclined."

Arthur looked to Sophronia. "Soph, would you mind terribly if I did not escort you home, but instead chaperoned Miss Audet? That is, if I can safely entrust you to the aegis of this rascal, whose character you surely know more intimately than I."

To her astonishment, Sophronia found herself relishing this cavalier dismissal by her beau. "No, Arthur, I don't mind. I assume we'll see each other at lunch on Monday, when we can talk more about this affair."

"Of course."

And with that, Arthur offered his arm to Fannie, and they strolled off.

Even in the dim illumination afforded by semi-remote gas fixtures in the street, Sophronia could detect in Reuben

Standeven's eyes a sparkle of excitement, pleasure, and joy at the prospect of this adventure.

And perhaps, Soph imagined, there was also showing a scintilla of eagerness, hesitation and trepidation, a smidgen of self-doubt as to how Sophronia would respond to their forced impulsive pairing? Could it be that Mister Standeven was not quite so cocksure and arrogant as she had always surmised? And that he held some regard for her sensibilities and judgments and – and her affections?

But any new respect for her coworker that might have been aborning was instantly put to flight by Reuben's words and actions.

Employing his rolled up broadside, he whapped her on the rump and said, "Quit your wool-gathering, Sappho! We've an investigation afoot!"

Sophronia prepared to let loose a rebuff as rude as Reuben's assault, when she halted herself and simply said, "Lay on, Macduff, and damn'd be him that first cries, 'Hold, enough!'"

SIX
IN THE CLUTCHES OF KNYGATHIN ZHAUM

Attaining the Power Street sidewalk which led uphill from South Main, Sophronia and Reuben began to ascend alongside the theatre, amidst the shadows cast by large luxuriant trees. No one else was in sight, and the cricket-filled June night seemed reserved just for them.

Sophronia suddenly realised that she was not even perturbed by Reuben inserting himself into her assignment. Somehow she did not mind his accompanying her on this mission.

"How did you become an intelligencer?" Sophronia found herself making this query almost without volition. Now why, especially at this odd juncture, should she suddenly be interested in the background of Reuben Standeven?

"An intriguing tale, one full of the most bathetic melodrama, which I shall mostly elide. As I approached my majority, I quickly discerned that journalism was the only profession open to me where I did not have to break my back and acquire a thick set of calluses, and which suited my peculiar talents. You see, I was an orphan from a very young age. My parents both died in the Great Revere Train Wreck, and no other relatives stepped forward to claim me. So by the age of eight I was living rough on the streets of Woonsocket, facilitated by charm and guile. Among a hundred petty larcenies, I carried gossip to earn my living. Utilised a facile tongue and nimble wit to escape injury and sustain myself. One day I suddenly asked myself: *what better combination of talents, experience and motivations than those for a journalist?* Oh, yes, and very little formal education. That's a definite plus. No book-fashioned set of blinders to obscure my perceptions of reality."

Sophronia humphed. "Your denunciation of institutional schooling is inaccurate. I myself can serve as a refutation of your premise. I am shaped by many years of formal instruction at St. Mary's Seminary, and yet I still see the lineaments of existence most clearly."

"Oh, you're pretty sharp, I grant you that. Not much escapes you, although you might not always put an accurate interpretation on matters, being too concerned with what the experts say. But we could still have a debate on your general perspicacity, at least in one area."

"And that realm would be?"

"Your boyfriend. What a nincompoop and duffer! Surely, despite his cold-fish nature, you must be blinded by passion, or you'd see him for the boring cipher he is."

Sophronia winced at this characterisation of Arthur, which came all too close to several intermittent misgivings of her own. But she could hardly align herself with such a slur.

"Mister Standeven, you have seen my beau Arthur for all of five minutes, and exchanged no more than a few words with him. How could you pass such a harsh judgment from that slight acquaintance?"

"It's as I said. I've got street-savvy that you can't pick up at St. Mary's out of books. It helps me immeasurably in my job, and

42

it's something you've got to acquire, or you'll never make the grade."

Sophronia felt that there was some truth to Reuben's assertion – outside of her romantic life, at least. "I do want more vital experiences, you know. I'm not scared or shy! I try to get Mister Callender to give me more meaty assignments. Not just the scientific beat, but rough-and-tumble stuff. But he won't!"

"Well, I'm sure he likes you okay. But you are a female. And so you are just going to have to work twice as hard to convince him you've got what it takes."

At this moment, the pair reached the rear upper corner of the theatre. A slate path led at right angles from the sidewalk to the rear door of the building, set in the middle of the windowless wall. Barely visible in the darkness, the door seemed securely shut.

Reuben put a finger to his lips, indicating silence. Taking Sophronia by the hand – a tingle of excitement accompanied his touch – and leading the way, he brought them to the door.

Sophronia reached past him to try the handle first. "Locked!" she softly exclaimed.

Reuben said nothing, but removed a large pocket-knife from his coat. Deft manipulation with its unfolded blade did the trick. In a moment, he had the door open.

"There was not a single bakery nor butcher shop in all of Woonsocket immune to my midnight incursions," he whispered, before ushering Sophronia inside.

Some faint radiance from outside perfused the interior through grimy windows. From what Sophronia could make out, this upper level of the building, above the auditorium, seemed to consist of corridors and modest rooms. Dim rubbishy shapes, as of forgotten costumes and props, lined the walls. How to descend to the stage below was a puzzle.

But then the immediacy of that task and its fulfilment was rendered secondary by the muted sound of voices. Hadn't they seen all the acolytes leave as they locked up? But could that nonetheless mean that *she* remained behind?

Sophronia instantly darted towards the exit, but was restrained by Reuben's hand on her wrist. He put his lips right next to her ear, and his warm breath made her quiver.

"You'll never reach your goal if you take flight at the first obstacle. Come on! Follow me!"

Reuben began to catfoot down the dark corridor toward the source of the ongoing conversation. Nerving herself up, Sophronia followed.

They rounded a corner and saw lamplight spilling out a partially opened office door. Reuben inched closer than Sophronia found comfortable, but she forced herself to match his boldness. Now the dialogue issuing from the unseen room could be easily interpreted.

The first voice was unmistakeably that of Isadora Blank, Hierophant of the Starry Sodality.

"I must insist, Zhaum, on you redoubling your efforts to close that trans-planar flaw. Why the rift had to be opened in the first place, I will never understand."

When it came, the voice of Blank's interlocutor was like no voice Sophronia had ever heard. Comparisons proved impossible to summon. It possessed attributes of an active gravel crusher, a wet sponge passing through a mangle, and a dog cracking a bone for its marrow.

"I needed sustenance and consultation."

"All very well. But then to let the portal drift away like that!"

"It wanders. Because of conditions at the other end."

"Yes, yes, I comprehend the astral weathers of Ulthar as well as you."

Ulthar! Sophronia could hardly believe her ears. Were these people discussing the mythical destination of lost cats as if it were real? What possible connection could there be between that plague of disappearances and the Sodality? But Isadora Blank's next words seemed to confirm the identity of one Ulthar with the other.

"All these terrestrial cats seem to have no trouble finding the rift. And their absence is arousing suspicions. Some people who know too much are putting the word about, even if only in chalked inscriptions. We need to shut this down, or it will interfere with our big day."

"Do not chide nor lecture me. I know as much as you. In fact, I know more."

"Such as?"

"That there are two intruders just outside this room!"

And faster than Sophronia or Reuben could react, the door of the office slammed wide open and a massive bulk hurled itself upon them like an avalanche!

Before they could even flinch, they had been snaffled. Sophronia felt herself being lifted off her feet and carried away, as her dress, gripped at the rear neckline, strained under her arms.

In the next second, squinting against the increased illumination from two wall-mounted gaslights, Sophronia found herself in the room whence the voices had issued, once more firmly planted on her feet. Reuben took a couple of staggering steps as he was set down more rudely.

Sophronia understood in an instant that the place was being used as a bedchamber, for an old canopied bedstead

45

predominated, with disarrayed coverlets. At its foot, a pallet of rags, furs, raw cotton batting, straw and string, formed into a curious nest – for a dog perhaps? A wardrobe with open doors revealed an array of conventional female garments.

And then Sophronia's attention was riveted by the people, one familiar, one supremely strange.

The familiar form and face belonged to Isadora Blank. Still clad in her flowing oracle's negligee, Isadora seemed slightly less glamorous than she had onstage, perhaps due to proximity and to tiredness and irritation on the part of the Hierophant. But Sophronia also had a queer notion that the woman had been caught with public pretences relaxed, as if, prior to their arrival she had doffed some kind of mask or disguise, and only hurriedly repositioned it as the uninvited guests were dumped precipitously into her lap.

But all such speculations ceased when the second person hove into Sophronia's view from a position behind her and Reuben.

The abnormally thin fellow was nearly seven feet tall, and clad in a mustard-coloured silk vest over bare chest, whilst a set of ballooning rose-coloured pantaloons (bare bony and large-nailed feet poking out) concealed his lower portions, the whole outfit causing him to resemble a genie of myth. But this was no affable and boisterous, albeit mischievous spirit, as betokened by the funereal expression on his dour and elongated phiz. Utterly hairless, giving the remote and blasphemously caricatural suggestion of the shaven priest, he featured a blanched epidermis with mottled pigmentation like that of a huge boa. Mammoth hands obviously possessed enough strength to hoist Soph and Reuben simultaneously. Most startling was the manner in which he moved with an unctuous, verminous ease, exhibiting an undulant litheness and fluidity that seemed to hint at an inner structure and vertebration that were less than human – or, one might almost have said, a sub-ophidian lack of all bony framework. He seemed to slither rather than walk; and the very fashion of his jointure, the placing of knees, hips, elbows and shoulders, appeared arbitrary and factitious.

Before Sophronia could fully assimilate the inhuman creature's menacing carriage and mien, Isadora had rounded roughly on the pair.

"Who are you two? What are you doing in my temple? This space is protected by potent charms and guardians. You risk much by venturing in unbidden. What do you want? What are you seeking?"

While Sophronia was still grasping for a proper response, Reuben stepped forward – the big queer fellow sinuously shifted his posture, as if prepared to stymie an assault – and made a graceful bow. Straightening, Reuben spoke blithely, as if meeting an old pal on the streetcorner.

"It's like this, Miss Blank. We are two lowly scribblers with the local rag, the *Journal*. Reuben Standeven and Sophronia Tempest. Surely an estimable, well-informed lady such as yourself takes our premier publication to stay abreast of matters, and thus you've no doubt seen our names in print. Not that I mean to stake any claim to fame, just trying to provide our bona fides. But that's neither here nor there, except as a basis of our admittedly impolite breaching of your domain. You see, we were both in attendance at your stimulating lecture tonight, and were so moved that we wish to interview you for a feature story. Your background and mission, the philosophy of the Starry Sodality, the nature of your Chopmist commune. All the usual guff. I'm sure you've fielded such questions a hundred times before. But

47

not yet for the *Journal*. It could be most invaluable coverage in promoting your cause, and also a keen bit of fluff to delight our readers. I'm certain it would attract many new patrons to your endeavours. Now, having unanimously decided on this interview, the two of us were most excited and determined to carry it off right away, before our zest had a chance to dissipate, and while your performance was still fresh in our brainpans. We tried to make our way to see you downstairs, but the flood of people prevented us. Having been locked out by your bell-hoppers, we ventured to the rear of your establishment, where we found an open door, and made so bold as to enter. A little timorous, we hesitated just outside your door. We were just about to knock and venture inside when Gargantua here made free with our persons, without so much as a by-your-leave. And that, as the farmer's daughter said to the over-eager swain, is enough of that!"

Isadora Blank had untensed during Reuben's peroration, allowing a slight smile to brighten her lovely face, and Sophronia felt that her comrade's speech, more or less the truth, had succeeded in disarming her hostility. But the attitude of her companion was another matter.

"I don't believe them," said the giant in his ghoulishly resonant voice. "They smell of trouble. And that back door was not unlocked."

"Oh, but it was," said Reuben, and Soph could almost hear his unspoken codicil: *Once I had my way with it!*

Ignoring the giant as if he had no status, Reuben addressed Isadora alone. "Madam, I fear we have not been introduced to your compatriot. Does he speak for you?"

Isadora said, "Permit me to announce Knygathin Zhaum, my second-in-command. He bears a high rank in the Sodality, and offers much support and counsel to our endeavours. Mister

Zhaum hails from the headwaters of the Nile, where his long-isolated tribe has maintained immemorial rites and precepts, long forgotten by other races, which allow communication with trans-galactic and ultramundane forces."

"An impressive, albeit archaic *curriculum vitae*, to be sure. Always glad to meet a wild foreign visitor to Columbia's shores, however uncultured they might be." Here Reuben bowed satirically to Zhaum, and received a hideous glare in exchange. "Nonetheless, madam, I take it that you and you alone make the decisions here. So while giving all due deference to Mister Zhaum's mistaken prejudices about us, I hope to hear that you understand and perhaps even condone our forgivable trespass, and might consent to a good long chinwag – all at your convenience, of course."

Isadora Blank pinched her lower lip with delicate forefinger and thumb and furrowed her brow in a coquettish manner that roused Sophronia's disdain. Then the Hierophant answered, "Yes, Mister Standeven, you and your partner in crime are forgiven, and I will certainly agree to an interview at some less wearisome hour. Now, if the two of you would take your departure by the way you entered, I would be most grateful, as I have had a long day."

Sophronia could hardly believe that they were escaping scot-free like this. She had been harbouring vivid visions of their imminent strangulation at the hands of Knygathin Zhaum, and the disposal of their corpses into the Bay off a nearby South Water Street dock.

Reuben grabbed Sophronia by the wrist and hurried her off, calling our over his shoulder, "Reach us at the *Journal*'s offices to arrange a time, Miss Blank!"

Back out on Power Street, Sophronia felt she could breathe easily again. The whole contretemps inside the theatre began to seem like an opium dream. Could there really exist such an anomalous creature as Knygathin Zhaum?

As they walked away at a good pace, Reuben said, "You accounted well for yourself back there, Soph. It took some bravery not to squeal at the sight of that monster."

"Well, yes, I suppose I did hold my ground quite steadily. But you were rather masterful yourself."

To her surprise, Reuben halted the two of them then and swept Sophronia up in his arms. He squeezed her tight for a moment, before planting a chaste kiss on her forehead and releasing her.

"Mister Standeven! I understand your sense of relief, for I share it too! But was it really necessary to express your emotion in such a peremptory fashion?"

"Ah, Soph! What a girl you could be if you did not have an astrolabe in place of your heart!"

SEVEN
THE SAVANT OF THE STACKS

At the breakfast table Saturday morning in the warm and fragrant kitchen, Sophronia's sense of the unshakeable firmness of quotidian reality, a commonplace foundation to life that she had taken for granted during her entire two decades on the planet, had reasserted itself fully, leaving only the smallest scintilla of eeriness behind. Everything she had witnessed and undergone at the theatre last night was positively explainable by scientific logic. The magic lantern gimmickry of Isadora Blank. The freakish abnormalities of that poor soul Zhaum, who, having been born in a benighted portion of the globe, had never received the proper medical care for his congenital afflictions. All things which, in the light of day, did not seem scary or inexplicable one whit, no matter how disturbing they had been in the darkness. As young Bertha fussed with muffins and fruit salad; and as her father sketched designs for improving the Kendall Manufacturing Soapine wagon meant for the much-anticipated Trades Procession; and as her mother sought to clean out Oscar's grimy ears while he squirmed and groused, Sophronia felt enveloped in blissful domestic surety.

Perhaps the most disturbing remnant of the whole expedition was the ghostly sensation of Reuben Standeven's lips on her brow. The utter audacity of that rascal! A good thing he had not made any further advances of an amorous nature, right up to the moment when he brought her back to the door of 380 Broadway – although Sophronia had been anticipating such. Had she remonstrated sternly enough with him for his bravado? Or perhaps too sternly? After all, she did not want to come across as some kind of antiquated bluenose from another generation. And what was that nasty remark about having an astrolabe for a heart? The gall! They had parted with a certain restrained and embarrassed solemnity. Oh well, there would be time to gauge his reservoir of ardour when they next met at the office, and to decide whether to stimulate or stanch it.

Along those lines, Sophronia paused to consider how Arthur and Fannie might have fared together for the rest of their Friday evening. She had a hard time picturing that tawdry chanteuse and her prim boyfriend establishing any affinities. She resolved, however, not to twit Arthur about his squiring of Miss Audet when she and he met for lunch on Monday.

Released from his maternal toils, Oscar practically dove into his plate of food. (Today the Mellin's Biscuit had been surreptitiously chucked into the firebox of the stove.) When he surfaced for a moment, he said, "Hey, Sis, I figured out how I'm gonna find that Ulthar place. I'm just gonna set Clutterbuck loose and follow him all day. He'll lead me there!"

Sophronia experienced an instinctive shudder as she recalled Zhaum's crypt-like voice claiming he himself had impossibly been to Ulthar for 'sustenance and consultation'. If Oscar should run into him –

"How absolutely ridiculous! Following a cat around all day. You'd better not implement any such scheme, Oscar. You could end up someplace dangerous before you realised where you'd gotten to."

Minnie Tempest said, "Oh, Soph, let your brother be. He has to occupy himself somehow, and it sound harmless enough. Maybe Clutterbuck will lead him to the missing cats and he can claim a reward for their restoration."

"Yes!" exulted Oscar. "The Old Sleuth saves the day!"

Unable to explain the source of her worry, Sophronia remained silent.

When she had finished dining, she bade her parents goodbye, saying, "I'm off to see Professor Charnley. I'm not sure when I'll be home."

Minnie Tempest responded with only half her attention, for she was busy fishing out a scorched yet seemingly invincible biscuit from the firebox, where its repugnant smouldering smell had roused her interest.

"That's nice, dear."

Oscar had hightailed it off before any biscuit-burning accusations could be levelled.

Clarence Tempest said, "Say, isn't your Professor Charnley one of those learning-shovers who poke around in the life of the Sandwich Islanders and suchlike? Ask him if he's ever come across any queer customs relating to soap. I might be able to work a few of the more colourful bits into our float. Although the deadline is rushing at us."

Indeed, as Sophronia had witnessed in her daily duties at the *Journal*, the June twenty-third debut of the fancifully bedizened carriages of the various tradesmen, much anticipated by the public, was beginning to loom larger and larger in the consciousness of the entire state. Attendance by spectators would certainly be phenomenal, as the parade wended its way back and forth through the streets of the capital city.

"I'll do that, Papa, although I don't think Professor Charnley has necessarily paid much attention in his researches to such domestic concerns among savages. He's more interested in philosophical and religious matters."

Out on the street, Sophronia thought to open her reticule and make sure she had brought along the sheet of paper whereon she had tried to reconstruct Isadora Blank's strange invocation: *Ia, ia! Vulgtm something, something, something, uh'e wgah'n,* and so forth... Perhaps the Professor could make heads or tails of the gibberish, if indeed it was not just nonsense.

Once again, the day being fine, Sophronia set out on foot, enjoying the busy bustle of Broadway. A pleasant stroll of half an hour brought her across town to the base of College Hill: specifically, the corner of North Main and Waterman, where reared the impressive wooden-framed, high-steepled First Baptist Church. The steep and winding ascent of Waterman Street did not daunt her, and she passed several other labouring pedestrians in her youthful vigour.

At the crest of the hill, Waterman was intersected by Prospect Street. And there on the northeast corner stood her destination: Brown University's New Library.

The strikingly handsome building had been completed just eight years ago, when the University had outgrown its Manning Hall library. After all, thirty thousand volumes was an enormous set of holdings that deserved uncramped quarters. And so this brick Gothic-Venetian building had been erected, one of the most advanced bibliotheque designs in the nation. Its floorplan basically mimicked a Greek cross whose three octagonal wings lent it the semblance of a cathedral.

Here Professor Aurion Charnley was mostly to be found, when he was not engaged in actual teaching. He had an official office elsewhere, but never used it. Likewise, he must certainly possess, surmised Soph, a residence somewhere on the East Side, but probably used that only for sleeping and eating his bachelor meals. Basically, he lived in the library. Sophronia had once asked him what attracted him to these odd quarters, aside from the obvious easy access to all the school's tomes.

"It's the cruciform construction," he replied. "Very protective. Also, my eyrie allows me to watch the horizons. Extremely valuable, you know, to have an early alert as to who or what might be visiting our fair city."

A typically eccentric response, but charming, she thought.

Sophronia glanced up at the large octagonal cupola that crowned the building, and thought to see movement behind one of its many windows.

She crossed the street and climbed the short flight of steps to the front door of the New Library. On this doorstep she invariably recalled an enigmatic comment Charnley had once made. Soph had remarked on the fact that to inaugurate the institution, Librarian Reuben Aldrich Guild had ceremoniously carried the first book into the new building, a copy of Samuel Bagster's *Polyglot Bible*. Charnley had snorted, then said, "Yes, that's the official story. But the first volume brought across the threshold was actually much older, and penned by a mad Arab." But when Sophronia inquired about the book's title, Charnley changed the subject and thereafter refused to acknowledge the matter.

Entering, Sophronia received a smile and nod from the majordomo at his station. Scattered tables and chairs occupied a capacious multi-storey rotunda that allowed access to the railed alcoves and their stacks. Six hundred gas lights ensured plenty of illumination for scholars.

Sophronia took the stairs and soon found herself on the third and penultimate level. No students or teachers were in evidence on this weekend summer day. There, bunching her skirts to achieve freedom of movement, she had to ascend an inconspicuous wall-mounted ladder to reach the cupola. At the top of the ladder she knocked on a trap door. Receiving acknowledgement to proceed, she pushed the hinged panel upward and climbed through.

Professor Charnley had his eye pressed to a small telescope aimed to the west. He continued to stare while Sophronia marvelled at the wealth of papers, books and odd souvenirs of the savant's extensive travels that filled nigh to bursting the shelves and other horizontal and vertical surfaces of the relatively small space. She picked up a strangely incised box which, upon being opened, revealed only a dusty stone trapezohedron.

Charnley pulled himself away from the eyepiece. A gnomish, cherubic fellow with a monk's tonsure of fluffy white hair and a rubicund complexion, Charnley sported, as always, a tobacco-ash-stained knitted vest, woollen trousers and dingy shirt with frayed cuffs.

Seeing the box in Sophronia's hands, he said, "Please put that down gently, Miss Tempest. That artifact is, ah, somewhat liable to mutability."

Soph did as asked. Since the Professor did not allude to their six-months' separation, neither did she. Truthfully, she always felt upon seeing him that they had only just parted.

"What were you observing, Professor?"

"Saint John's Church on Federal Hill. There have been some baffling quasi-celestial phenomena centred there of late. But for now, things seem quiet."

Soph admired the panoramic view which included a large swath of Narragansett Bay as well as the leafy city. "Well, you're certainly emplaced perfectly to catch anything that happens in your wide vista. And speaking of strange phenomena, allow me to relate what just occurred to me last night."

Soprhonia gave a detailed account of the doings at the theatre. Charnley listened with growing intensity and interest.

"'Ulthar' was mentioned, you say? And coincident with this civic cat affair... Let me see that transcription you made."

Sophronia dug out the paper with Isadora Blank's meaningless syllables.

As Charnley let his eye rove over the fragmentary words, his expression became more and more concerned. Looking up, he said, "This is a deeper affair than you might at first conceive, my dear. If you could possibly recall more of this woman's speech... No? Well then, I shall just have to proceed with what we have. I suspect my investigations will take at least a day or two. Suppose you return here on Tuesday? But meanwhile, I would advise you to steer clear of these folks. They are not necessarily whom they represent themselves to be. That Zhaum fellow in particular. Your description of him tallies more with a Hyperborean origin than any natal genesis in Ethiopia or the Sudan."

Sophronia rewarded Professor Charnley with a peck on his cheek (the innocent gesture instantly recalled to her Reuben Standeven's more daring kiss), and exited the cupola with all due care for the awkward intersection of rungs and skirts.

The rest of her Saturday, Sophronia devoted to shopping, acquiring several new outfits at Edward C. Almy & Co., as well as some reagents for her basement chemistry lab, while mentally rehearsing the article she would write in fulfilment of her assignment from editor Mack Callender. There was no point in turning in an incomplete draft. She would have to delay until Charnley finished his researches into the matter, which she would incorporate into her piece, if they merited.

At home, Sophronia was half-expecting to hear from Arthur. After all, he had mentioned that he wanted to take in the new performers at the San Souci Gardens. But he never called on her, and she was not about to go running after him. Anyway, it was more pleasant to relax at home with a brand-new novel, recommended by one of her girlfriends from St. Mary's: *Atla: The Story of the Lost Island*, by Ann Eliza Smith. A little more fanciful than the lectures of Michelson, but a nice change of pace from her usual lucubrations.

Retiring to her chambers past midnight, when everyone else in the house was fast asleep, Sophronia received a horripilating scare when she glanced at her uncurtained bedroom window and thought to see a mottled white inhuman face floating outside. Instantly she thought of Knygathin Zhaum, and, heart palpitating, snatched up a heavy brass candlestick as a weapon. But upon a second look, no face was apparent. And of course, how could there be, given that her bedroom was on the third floor, with no porch or other means of access? This could only have been a phantasm engendered by her unwonted fantastical reading.

Sunday proved a very quiet and relaxing day, with church services and visits from neighbours and friends, along with an elaborate midday feast. Oscar chafed in his fancy suit, but behaved himself for a change, until freed to roam in the afternoon.

On Monday Sophronia headed into the *Journal* offices. She had crafted an entire dialogue between herself and Reuben Standeven, with numerous alternate branchings, but it never got deployed, for he was out on an assignment. Mack Callender was so preoccupied with news emanating from the kingdom of Buganda, about the slaughter of some Christian converts, that he only half-listened to her excuses about why she was not ready yet with her article on the Starry Sodality.

"By jingo, how I wish I were in the field again! I'd wring the truth out of that weasel of a Nubian King!"

At lunchtime, with a sigh, Sophronia set out for Warren & Wood Crockery to meet with Arthur.

Upon entering the establishment, she was greeted with an inexplicable cascade of sniggers and half-suppressed jibes from Arthur's co-workers who knew her. Shrugging off the juvenile japery as simply an excess of Two Hundred and Fiftieth Anniversary high spirits, she went in search of her boyfriend. But he was nowhere to be found, and she finally had to inquire in the offices.

The secretary, a famously gruff, tight-collared fellow who nonetheless seemed to show some sympathy today, broke the news to Soph.

"Mister Botwink did not arrive to work this morning, and in fact has seen fit to tender his resignation from the firm in the form of this here mentally deviant telegram."

He handed Sophronia the paper form.

FOUND SALVATION STOP GONE TO LIVE AT THE S.S. COMMUNE STOP REACH OUT FOR THE CONSTELLATIONS AND LIVE STOP

EIGHT
AT THE COMMUNE OF THE BLACK GOAT

Early Tuesday morning, June eighth, found a certain distinctive conveyance outbound from Providence along the Danielson Pike, its nonobvious destination the Commune of the Black Goat, in the vicinity of Chopmist Hill, Scituate. The vehicle was a standard Rockaway carriage – roofed seat for the driver, a cabin to hold six – drawn by a spirited bay stallion and painted gaudily in yellow and black, bearing the legend of *The Manufacturers and Farmers Journal* on its doors. It was in fact the official transportation utilised by Sophronia's employer for various functions and errands, and its loan had been secured with no small amount of cajolery directed at Soph's boss. In this effort she had, most gratifyingly, been aided by her coworker, Reuben Standeven. Together they had made the case to Mack Callender that the Starry Sodality deserved further investigation, since it had proven to be able to command a large following among the state's citizenry, even unto the point of establishing a cooperative agricultural enterprise. Eventually Callender had agreed, saying, "Just make sure you come back with some solid facts about their backers and credo and such. I won't be lulled into printing mere speculations."

And although Sophronia did firmly intend to dig into the reasons for the sect's popularity and their seemingly impossible plans to abandon terrestrial life for some far off nebulous Arcadian realm – mainly by quizzing Isadora Blank deeply, should she find her, on the sect's property, as she hoped – her main purpose in visiting the so-called Commune of the Black Goat was to try to discover whatever had got into Arthur Botwink to transform him from a sober-sided jug peddler to an irresponsible lotus eater, and, if possible, to reclaim him for sanity.

Her journalistic companion in this outing, Reuben Standeven, had much the same mixture of motives, since, in a disclosure made later that Monday, it eventuated that his ex-companion, Miss Fannie Audet, erstwhile chanteuse, had, with identical precipitousness, tossed aside her old life and also gone over to the Starry Sodality cause.

After discovering this unlikely happening, Reuben had exclaimed to Soph, "This is a woman who has to have her nightly calf's milk bath with violet-scented *sels aromatiques*! I can't picture her grubbing about among the turnips while chanting a hymn to Osiris, or whoever these Milky Way-obsessed clodpolls worship."

Sophronia replied, "And as for Arthur, I've seen him nearly reduced to tears by the proximity of an over-aggressive hornet."

Indeed, the pair of baffled reporters agreed, there must exist some powerful allure or stimulus to have attracted such unlikely recruits to the pastoral life.

Monday's lunchtime revelation of her fiancé's utter abandonment of his old life had initially sent Sophronia straight home from the Crockery concern, seeking advice from her mother. To her surprise, Minnie Tempest was already consoling Charity Botwink, Arthur's plump mother, anent this very same topic, and so no further explanation of the unprecedented situation had to be made. After listening to an hour or so of repetitive maternal commiseration – "But he was always such a *good* boy!" "I know, dear, I know, but we can never tell what secret springs may be bubbling under." – Sophronia had her fill of useless weeping, and so returned to the *Journal* offices. There she had received Reuben's information about Fannie Audet.

"What are we going to do about this?" she demanded of Reuben.

"Plainly, we need to speak to both of our straying lambs, and convince them of the folly of their ways. I stress that I am not Fannie's caretaker, nor even her steady flame. Yet I feel some responsibility to help her. Your case is somewhat more weighty and imperative. Although why you'd actually want Arthur back –"

"Just stop it. What if we fail to persuade them?"

"I don't know. Maybe we can shanghai them both. A cosh behind the ear, and bango!"

"I would prefer not to be known as a woman who secures the attentions of her straying paramour with a 'cosh behind the ear'."

"As you wish. Although such a reputation, I imagine, might be very useful at times. But hark, we have to get out to Scituate anyhow to accomplish anything. That's the first step. So let's brace old Mack for some help."

And so it was that Tuesday's dawn saw Reuben and Sophronia on the road.

But not alone, for two other members of the expedition had been arranged.

The first addition had been insisted on by Callender.

"I'm not entrusting the *Journal*'s exclusive carriage to a couple of youthful culverheads and gumsuckers such as you two. So you'll take a driver. Crispus Bannister is his name. You might have heard of his cousin, Edward Bannister, the famous painter."

"Yes, of course," said Reuben. "That black Barbadian who now resides here in the state."

"A Negro driver sounds fine," said Sophronia. "I've known many such wonderful men. Just so long as he won't be affrighted by anything unnatural we might encounter."

Callender laughed. "Do you recall that incident in the North Burial Grounds a few years ago, when some fellow claiming to be a wizard was digging up fresh graves? Crispus helped catch him by waiting up all night every night for a week among the lonely, looming monuments. No, he'll be quite unflappable."

The fourth member of their jaunt had enrolled himself, under the name of Professor Aurion Charnley.

Monday night found Sophronia in the kitchen, cooking up enough food for their journey. Chopmist Hill was some eighteen miles from Providence, and the ride out would occupy four or five hours, with, logically, a return trip of equal duration. Nothing else about the mission might be under her control, but she did not have to rely on chancy victuallers.

Sophronia heard the doorbell ring while she was blotting excess lard from her buttermilk fried chicken. Minnie Tempest pushed through the kitchen door almost instantly thereafter, trailed by a most unlikely figure: Professor Charnley! He looked so anomalous out of his eyrie that Soph took a moment to fully recognise him. She had completely forgotten their appointment for the morrow.

"My dear," said the gnomish savant, "I am so glad to find you safe and sound. The things I've discovered about your Miss Blank and her crowd! Very disconcerting, very, even if I can't be one hundred percent certain about their origins and intentions. I'm here to offer my services in dealing with them. I feel I might have a few aces up my sleeve that you do not. So the next time you confront them, I'd like to accompany you."

"But this is marvellous! We go to beard them in their den tomorrow!"

After hearing the story of Arthur and Fannie, Professor Charnley said, "Perfect! I'll meet you at the appointed hour at the *Journal* offices."

And so it came to pass that at roughly eleven AM on that Tuesday, after four hours of travel down bucolic country roads – such a welcome respite from the hurly-burly of the Providence metropolis! – the black and yellow carriage could be found parked at the intersection of the Danielson Pike and Chopmist Hill Road. The spot was a shady one and featured a low stone wall on which the quartet of travellers sat, and on which was spread a chequered cloth and a large hearty collation.

Reuben and the Professor, meeting for the first time back in the city, had hit it off like old pals.

"I must say, Professor Charnley, that I was much taken with your paper on the myths of sunken cities among the Pacific islanders. It read in parts like a Nick Carter adventure."

Reuben's familiarity with any such scholarly work – even if only its dime novel aspects – raised him up in Sophronia's estimation, and she eyed him with fresh appreciation.

Before responding, Charnley hoisted into the carriage a heavy satchel whose mysterious contents he would not disclose. "Please, my boy, call me Aurion. Did you really like that little essay? I do think it represents some very original work, if I say so myself."

As for Crispus Bannister, a burly fellow with more white than black in his close-cropped hair and beard, all three travellers felt an instant affinity with his no-nonsense aura of competence. A twinkle in his eyes somewhat belied the sternness of his visage.

"Mack explained to me," said Crispus after introductions, "that we all might encounter some resistance or even downright hostility from these folks we're going to meet. So I saw fit to bring along old Bessie."

From its long oiled sheath, Crispus slid partially out a rifle that seemed only slightly shorter than Sophronia herself.

"Good Lord," said Reuben, "what kind of monstrous weapon is that?"

"A Nitro Express elephant gun, imported from England. I probably would've brung it along even if we weren't planning to interrogate this pack of loonies you describe. Those Swamp Yankees out in Scituate and Foster and Chepachet are all disagreeable, ornery and touchy cusses. Look at that there Dorr Rebellion back in 'forty-two, centred right in Chepachet. Prickly about strangers, and positively anti-officialdom. Them folks just don't take to city types poking their noses into their rural doings."

After their long ride, wherein lots of pleasant chatter had further cemented the impromptu bonds among the quartet, with Crispus chiming in from his exterior seat, their picnic proved a further agreeable interlude of idle conversation. No one really wanted to speculate on what might await them at the Commune of the Black Goat, and Professor Charnley had not gone into details about his findings concerning the Starry Sodality. All he had said was, "These people, I have reason to believe, are in league with entities and forces they cannot possibly hope to control. It's a matter of not raising up things you can't put down."

Sophronia asked, "Do you mean actual supernatural beings and powers? You know I don't credit such things."

"No, not at all. Your faith in science can and should remain unshaken, my dear. I mean cosmic realities which are as much a part of the natural universe as you or I, but representative of precincts where perhaps the very laws of physics differ from what we know. Alien mentalities, a kind of cosmically cold and horrifying set of perspectives. Working through Isadora Blank and company, they mean to accomplish something. But precisely what, I cannot venture yet to say."

This nebulous declaration naturally caused Soph and Reuben to worry further about the toils in which their friends had gotten themselves enmeshed.

Eventually all of the food reserved for their first meal had been consumed with enjoyment. Reuben had remarked, "My god, this chicken could take a prize! Soph, you prove yourself not only a whiz of a scribbler, but a consummate kitchen angel. He who has you for a helpmeet someday may account himself a lucky man."

This praise caused Sophronia to blush, and she could only pooh-pooh it.

After turning onto Chopmist Hill Road the company found themselves in a district of widely separated farm houses of antique and impoverished mien, hunkered down amidst scrubby vegetation and looking more like excrescences of the soil than manmade structures. The road steadily ascended, for Chopmist Hill was the highest point in the town of Scituate, and indeed one of the highest elevations in the whole state.

Before too much longer they arrived at their destination, foreknown from inquiries made at the Scituate Town Hall.

The Commune of the Black Goat had once been, ironically, the headquarters of the Second Free Will Baptist Society, until the decades-long decay, dwindling and dissolution of that flock. An estate composed of one large hip-roofed house displaying peeling paint, and numerous straggling, shoddy outbuildings, the whole assemblage sat on the naked crown of Chopmist Hill. Seeing the place, Sophronia was struck with an anomalous sensation. Although the day was bright and mild, it seemed as if the whole place were helplessly exposed to the naked black interstellar realms lying just beyond the duplicitous blue sky.

A few tethered horses and a buggy betokened the presence of at least some persons, but no one was visible. A lone black goat, far from eldritch in its manner or behaviour, cropped the weeds of its namesake territory.

Crispus parked their carriage and descended from his perch, while Soph, Reuben and the Professor disembarked – the last-named clutching his satchel. Their driver unlimbered his Nitro Express rifle and said, "I'll wait here, to watch our ride. Just holler if you need me."

Feeling somehow responsible for bringing Reuben and Professor Charnley to this unlikely camp, Sophronia strode bravely in the advance of their little party towards the house. But before she could venture inside, the sound of a familiar female voice emanating from outdoors, to the rear of the house, made her correct her course.

Behind the main building, a strange scene awaited.

A dozen acolytes of the Starry Sodality, men and women of varied sorts, all clad in plain robes, sat cross-legged on the weedy lawn. Eagerly, Sophronia sought out Arthur's face, but found him not – nor Fannie Audet either.

Sitting likewise on a cushioned dais was Isadora Blank. Even in the light of day, the Hierophant retained the ineffable glamour she had exhibited onstage under beguiling gas light. Her russet locks lent her a leonine air, and the suggestive lineaments of her ripe body beneath gossamer fabric conveyed a lush carnal abandonment.

Imperturbable, Isadora Blank finished her address to her disciples before acknowledging the visitors.

"You must first ascend your inner chakras, before you will be qualified to ascend to the stars. Focus and concentrate! Visualise the progression of your wisdom up the column of your spine. You must transcend the merely human! Repeat to yourself these words from the *Bhagavat Geeta*: 'I am the ritual and the sacrifice. I am the womb and the eternal seed.' Now, practice your discipline until I return."

Unfolding herself gracefully, Isadora Blank stepped down from the platform – Sophronia noted it was simply a homely carpet atop some boards atop some hay bales – and gestured her visitors to follow her. Once around the corner of the house, where they would not distract the disciples, the priestess turned to them and smiled graciously.

"Miss Tempest, Mister Standeven, how good to see you again. And do my eyes detect that fabled expert on all things anthropological, Professor Charnley of Brown University?"

The professor nodded solemnly. "I claim no particular distinctions, Miss Blank. I am merely a student of human behaviours, here to assist my friends in their interrogations."

"So I am to assume that you two reporters are here to conduct that interview I promised."

Sophronia said, "Yes, of course. But we had also hoped to have a look about your establishment. Is your entire congregation busy with their, um, chakras, or are there other members present?"

"Oh, no, we have additional followers. They are busy in the fields. We alternate manual and spiritual labours here, to improve the whole person."

"Might we see them before we indulge in our dialogue?"

"Of course. Just go right over the crest of the hill. Your momentary diversion will allow me to complete the training session. Then we'll talk inside."

Sophronia and her friends left the Hierophant behind.

Reaching the high point of the property, they were presented with an unforeseen sight, formerly concealed.

An acre or two of sloping land had been furrowed and planted. But the crop bore no resemblance to any plant Sophronia knew. The dirt rows were occupied by ranks of globular fungoid masses, about shin-high, looking like black truffles or perhaps undersea brain corals.

Hoeing weeds were another dozen acolytes.

And watching over them, like some plantation overseer, was Knygathin Zhaum. Still wearing his djinn's suit, Zhaum struck Soph like the Simon Legree of some foreign clime.

Zhaum regarded them coolly, but made no move to interfere with their visit.

Now Sophronia spotted Arthur, and beside him Fannie Audet, both berobed as disciples. She hastened over to the pair, her comrades following.

"Arthur! Whatever can have possessed you to flee to this impossible place, and put yourself under the tutelage of this – this witch! You must come back to Providence with us immediately! Your parents are beside themselves."

Arthur appeared flustered yet adamant, fully himself, albeit exhibiting different beliefs than normal, yet with no signs of being mesmerised or coerced.

"Sophronia, I appreciate your concern and the efforts you have made to track me down. But my mind is made up. I have cast my lot with the Sodality, in hopes of a more glorious future life among the stars. I would like for you too to join us, but I suspect that your nature is too sceptical. So all I ask is to be left alone to pursue my destiny."

Sensing that argument would only harden her fiancé's position, Soph said, "Arthur, please think carefully for the next hour or three upon your choices. We will be leaving then, and there's plenty of room in our carriage for two more. Perhaps Miss Audet could likewise be swayed to come home, if that's what's holding you here."

But Fannie Audet had been unswayed by Reuben's similar implorings. "Rube, honey, it's not that we ain't had some nanty narking together. It's just that this here is where my soul has come to rest – and I never even knew till now that I had one!"

Soph noticed that Reuben's hand was ready to withdraw something from his pocket – possibly the aforementioned cosh – but she shook her head in the negative, rolling her eyes towards that fearsome scarecrow, Zhaum. Reuben sighed, then released his grip on the blackjack.

Reluctantly then, Soph turned aside from her beau and walked disconsolately away. Zhaum glared at them, but did not pursue or threaten.

Back at the house, Soph found the class dismissed. Venturing warily inside, the party came upon Isadora Blank ensconced on a couch in the shabbily furnished first-floor parlour, which housed what had to be the remnant chairs and tables, framed lithographs and bookcases from the Baptist heyday. Although her mind and heart were preoccupied with Arthur's condition and contrariness, Soph forced herself to assume a reportorial professionalism. With Reuben's aid, she began to conduct an interview with the priestess, although with only half her attention.

Her notes later revealed a colourful farrago of imprecise and hazy allusions to distant countries, training by secret masters, a humble apprenticeship, aspirations to spiritual transcendence, and a desire for the betterment of the whole human race. It was a beguiling fairytale that went down easily while in progress, but showed itself full of holes afterwards – at least to Soph's sceptical mind.

Finally Soph's questions and probes petered out, having broken themselves against the bland impenetrable walls of Isadora Blank's fortress of generalities.

Only then, as she looked up from her pad and pencil, did Sophronia notice that Professor Charnley was missing. She became alarmed, but tried to maintain her sangfroid.

"Well, Miss Blank, I expect we have enough information now for our piece on the Starry Sodality. Isn't that right, Mister Standeven?"

Reuben was scratching his head like a burglar stymied by an uncrackable safe. "I guess so. Can we return if we have more questions, or even see you in town?"

"Of course. I'd be delighted."

The priestess conducted them out the front entrance.

Soph's heart jumped for joy when she saw, first, Crispus Bannister vigilant by their coach, and then Professor Charnley, standing by an adjacent barn. The professor's beckoning stance plainly indicated he wished them to join him, and so they did, with Isadora seemingly unruffled.

"Miss Blank," said Charnley, "may I ask what this is?"

He swung open the barn doors.

Inside was a huge wagon, a mighty dray. It featured an outlandish simulacrum of some kind of never-neverland, a wild and tangled alien landscape scaled down to fit the bed of the wagon. Gnarled trees, grasping lianas and half-seen monsters, all fashioned of some malleable material and painted in the most eye-straining colours.

"Oh, this little thing," said Isadora lightly, "is to be our surprise entry into the Trades Procession on the twenty-third. We felt that as one of the newer enterprises in the city, we might attempt to make a paltry showing amongst the other more established concerns. I hope you won't give away our small surprise, Professor. Do you like our creation? It's meant to resemble the jungles of Abbith, a world around the star of Xoth."

"Yes, I recognised it as such. Generally regarded as a rather inhospitable place, I think."

Isadora Blank smiled. "To some, assuredly. To others, not."

The priestess saw them back to their carriage then.

Sophronia strained her gaze one final time towards the truffle fields, but was not rewarded with any last-minute appearance by Arthur or Fannie. Reluctantly, she and the others boarded the carriage, and Crispus rolled them safely away.

All dispirited and meditative, no one said anything for the length of their travel down Chopmist Hill Road. The remaining journey back to the city stretched away like a funeral. As they approached the intersection where they had enjoyed lunch – seemingly a happier eternity ago – Sophronia was about to speak.

But a sudden act of violence intervened!

As evidenced by noise and jolting, their horse must have reared up, neighing wildly and nearly upsetting the coach.

Crispus' commands rang out and established some obedience over the nervous steed as they came to a juddering halt.

Sophronia stuck her head out one window. Motion drew her eye upward, and she saw the impossible.

In the sky was an enormous bat-winged wraith, a thing of grey parchment skin stretched over bizarre musculature and misarticulated bones. Its feet and hands were equipped with razored claws. But most terribly, its horned head sported *no face*, just a blank façade! Nonetheless, it seemed to have no trouble zeroing in on their vehicle.

Not wishing to be trapped, Soph impulsively tumbled out of the carriage, falling to the ground. She sensed Reuben and the professor following close behind.

Its silence more frightening than any cries, the apparition swooped down upon her. Soph could feel the buffets from its wings, smell the hot summer dirt of the road. What a catalogue of final sensations!

An enormous blast from the elephant gun erupted, and Soph saw a gaping hole open up in the thing's midriff as it recoiled from the projectile. But there came no blood or kindred fluids, merely shreds of its otherworldly substance.

And that gaping hole now knitted itself together just as swiftly as it had formed!

Reuben stood bravely above Soph, his fists raised in a defensive gesture out of all magnitude to the threat.

The creature resumed its plummet.

And then came the voice of Professor Charnley, spewing out contorted syllables akin to those Isadora Blank had used in the theatre. Held aloft in the professor's hands glowed the very same trapezohedron that Soph had handled in his eyrie, the dull stone now enlivened!

The winged being tried to retreat, but too late. Momentum carried it into the swelling nimbus radiating from the shaped stone, and the flying monster evaporated like a soap bubble.

Reuben helped Sophronia to stand. Her legs felt quavery, but she forced herself to exude calmness.

"Reuben, your risked your life for me."

"No more than Crispus or the Prof did."

"I shan't forget any of it."

Reuben grinned. "I'll hold you that, and claim my share of the reward at some future date."

Their bewildered driver was staring at the gun in his hand and shaking his head. "I ain't never seen anything stand up to old Bessie like that. What in tarnation was it?"

The Professor was calmly restoring the trapezohedron to its special box. Once the box was latched, he said, "A night-gaunt. But I was ready for just such an eventuality. You apprehend better now, I think, what we are up against."

The rest of the trip home passed in relieved but dismal silence as Sophronia contemplated just what their fate might have been, had the professor not been so well prepared and equipped.

The path of their return to the city brought them first and most conveniently to 380 Broadway, around six PM. Uncertain about what might come next in their quest to unriddle the intentions of the Starry Sodality, Sophronia prepared to say thank you and goodbye to her comrades, and to arrange, at the very least, another meeting amongst themselves soon.

But as the carriage pulled up to Sophronia's home, her mother rushed out frantically, interrupting any attempt at planning.

75

"Soph, oh Soph, thank God you've returned! Your brother's gone missing since this morning. We need everyone to help find him! I can't bear to imagine him all lost and hurt!"

NINE
TO ULTHAR AND BEYOND!

Holding the Tempest family cat Clutterbuck firmly in the cradle of her arms, Sophronia examined the spot where the ginger tom had led her, before he had paused to sit and unconcernedly lick himself. Could this be the secret means of finding her lost brother? She dared to hope so, though she found it hard to believe that such a mundane place could furnish a clue to anywhere outré.

Soph stood in front of the famous drinking fountain that graced the sidewalk boundary of the Providence Athenaeum Library on Benefit Street, halfway up College Hill in the direction of Professor Charnley's hideout. Inside a decorative pillared arch carved in the granite wall, a plain metal pipe coursed forth delicious water that fell, first, into a carven clamshell, and thence into a large trough whose drain diameter was calculated nicely to prevent overflow but always leave a full reservoir. Inscribed under the top of the arch was the legend:

COME HITHER EVERY ONE THAT THIRSTETH.

Sophronia ran over once more the tangled sequence of events that had led her here on this early morning of Wednesday, June 9th.

When Minnie Tempest had feverishly accosted the returnees last night with news of Oscar's vanishing, all thoughts of the Starry Sodality had been instantly driven from her brain. And yet, as the dimensions and details of Oscar's disappearance had been revealed, Sophronia began to believe that the two were not unconnected.

For Oscar had vanished while embarked on his quixotic search for Ulthar, the same venue to which Knygathin Zhaum had once alluded.

This is what had happened, based on the collated and clarified reports from Oscar's pals who had been with him at the time of the enigmatic incident.

Yesterday morning after breakfast, while Sophronia was on the road to Scituate, Oscar had resumed his search for the passage to Ulthar, putative home of all the missing Providence cats. Failing to obtain results, he had grown tired of following Clutterbuck about the immediate neighbourhood, and so, putting the cat into a lidded pie basket (despite Oscar's sometimes rough treatment of the beast, it was generally mild and tractable, and even seemed to love the lad), Oscar had rounded up some fellows and headed down to the South Water Street docks. And there the mystery had occurred.

Setting Clutterbuck free, Oscar had followed the cat as it idled down the length of one pier, possibly trawling the scent of fish. At the end of that dock stood a small shack, no bigger than a privy. A smudged window afforded a view of the untenanted interior.

Oscar opened the door and entered with his cat.

The two had never exited.

When the other boys got tired of waiting, they opened the cabin door – the place had been under their observation the whole while – and found it empty. Baffled, they nevertheless did not think to tell the Tempest family until the lunch hour.

Upon receiving the shock, Minnie Tempest was immediately convinced that Oscar, who must have been spirited away through some impossibly concealed trapdoor in the shack and into a waiting boat, was on his way to the white-slave markets of the Orient.

The hue and cry was raised, and six hours later, upon Sophronia's return, all the vast efforts of the searchers had revealed nothing more about the affair.

Professor Charnley, Crispus and Reuben had instantly offered their services in the hunt.

"I have a certain scrying stone back at the library that might be of use," said the Professor, and departed.

"Let me return this here carriage," Crispus said, "and then I'll roust out some of the Snowtown folks to search."

"There must be a dozen of my cronies hanging out at Pickman's Ale House," said Reuben. "I'll give a cooey, and they'll come running!"

After her three friends departed, Soph realised that there was little aid she could offer in the way of physically canvassing the town, and so she took her mother's arm and ushered her inside. There the womenfolk spent a generally sleepless night, receiving reports from the various areas as they were combed, while subsisting on cookies, tea and cold ham sandwiches. (Bertha performed her extraordinary duties admirably, ceasing her continuous Nordic weeping for "poor little Oscar" at random intervals, whenever handsome young male searchers stopped in for a revivifying snack.)

Soph managed to catch a few winks here and there, so that when dawn broke she felt possessed of about a quarter of her usual energy – a miracle, especially considering the depletions wrought by the night-gaunt attack.

She ventured out onto the front stoop of 380 Broadway for a breath of fresh air. The street's normal activities went on as usual, just as if her brother were not vanished down a hole in the fabric of the universe.

Suddenly she felt something rubbing on her ankles.

Clutterbuck.

Soph snatched up the cat and rushed inside.

"Mother, Mother, look who's returned!"

Minnie Tempest was not as enthused as her daughter. "Oh, Soph, what does that matter? Of course Clutterbuck was not abducted. The white-slavers have no need for cats!"

At that moment, Clarence Tempest entered the house. He looked as if he had been dragged behind a runaway horse over six miles of gravel road.

"Papa, look, it's Clutterbuck!"

"Daughter, please, don't trouble me with inanities. I recognise our own cat, after all. I'm just back for some coffee before I go out again. We are arranging boats to drag the Cove. My God, how I wish I were dead, rather than be forced to utter that sentence with regard to my own flesh and blood! Moreover, a second calamity has struck our fair city. A universal, not personal calamity. Mayor Doyle has just died."

Even under their familial strain, Sophronia found resources within herself to sympathise with the dreadful news. The city's favourite son, beloved by all and reigning as mayor longer than any predecessor, he who had done so much to arrange the grand and glorious Two-Hundred-and-Fiftieth Anniversary celebrations, had not lived to see the joyful fruition. His predestined successor, Gilbert Robbins, was a fine man, but no paragon like Doyle. No greater tragedy since the burning of Roger Williams's settlement during King Phillip's War had ever happened! "What cheer, Netop?" now indeed!

Realising she could not convey to her parents the significance of Clutterbuck's manifestation – if he had indeed been to Ulthar, he was the only cat ever to return – Sophronia took the pet to her chambers. There she refreshed herself and changed clothes. Twenty-four hours in the same garments had left her feeling rather "ripe." Then, without speaking to anyone, she left the house, carrying the cat in a hatbox.

Lacking any more logical starting point, Sophronia commenced her search at the dock where Oscar had vanished. But Clutterbuck showed no interest in returning to the shack. Soph recalled how Knygathin Zhaum had remarked that the entrance to Ulthar wandered. Evidently, it was no longer here.

But Clutterbuck seemed to have some idea of its new location. Like a furry arrow, he had trotted as directly as possible from South Water to South Main and thence to the foot of College Street. Uphill alongside the flank of the large courthouse, and to a stop in front of the Athenaeum Fountain.

Now Sophronia wondered what came next.

Clutterbuck showed her.

He walked unhesitatingly into the granite wall that hosted the fountain just as if it were a mirage, or a magically painted scrim of smoke, his tail disappearing last.

Closing her eyes, Sophronia practically hurled herself after the cat, all the while expecting her face and bosom to smash against the unyielding stone.

But she encountered no such common sense barrier.

She opened her eyes.

Above her spread a velvety night sky mapped with an infinity of polychrome stars in no discernible constellations. So deep was it that for a moment Soph felt as if she were falling impossibly upward into the sidereal depths.

Something told her that it was always night here in this new dimension, that no sun ever rose and shone.

Drawing her gaze downward, Sophronia saw that she stood on the breast of a small hill, and that below her on the level ground, at no great remove, stretched a compact township, a thousand queer thatched cottages with lighted windows, with a few larger buildings interspersed along narrow and twisting cobbled roads. A somnolent snaking river bisected the town, with one distinctive elbow nearest to her, and somehow its name obtruded into Soph's brain: the Skai.

<<I must take my leave of you now.>>

She did not cognise those words as traditional verbal speech, but rather as some other form of information delivered down impalpable channels. She turned her head to view her interlocutor.

Clutterbuck stood bipedally, as large as his ex-mistress, so that he could stare eye-to-eye. His whiskers twitched as he spoke, and in some manner his muzzle conveyed a small smile.

<<I need to return to my wife and children,>> said the cat. <<Good luck finding your brother. Tell him he must eat his own vitamin biscuits from now on.>>

Clutterbuck strode manfully off, humming a gay tune.

Once she had recovered from her bewilderment, Sophronia followed down the dark grassy slope.

The cobbles of Ulthar's streets were slick with night dew. Sophronia walked carefully, lest she slip. She shared the roadways with humans – or what curiously passed for humans here in Ulthar – and of course with many human-sized cats, all perambulating proudly like Puss-in-Boots. Citizens of both these kinds acknowledged her presence politely, and yet Soph found herself reluctant to stop anyone from their busy rounds and make her queries.

Where is my brother?

What can you tell me of one Knygathin Zhaum and Isadora Blank, of the Starry Sodality and their plans?

Her wanderings up and down the byways of Ulthar seemed to go on forever. The changeless night afforded no metrics of time. She passed several taverns – or was it the same one, over and over? – which looked inviting enough and where she might have refreshed herself. But recalling the consequences for those who had wandered into Oberon's realm and eaten the food thereof, she declined any wordless invitations.

Her feet grew sore, her limbs heavy, her mind sluggish. She sat down on a horse-mounting stone outside a cobbler's. (DOUBLE PAWS OUR SPECIALTY.)

And along came two impossible creatures.

They looked like rolypoly men made of dough, as if someone had animated two obese clay Buddha statues.

<<What's this, what's this?>> said one.

<<I think it's a Thing from that world where the Yith rule.>>

<<The Yith! They've been extinct for a hundred and fifty million years!>>

83

<<Don't be dense or fractious! You know the place I mean, by any designation.>>

<<Oh please, sirs,>> said Soph, <<who are you? Can you help me find my brother, and learn what I need to know about some enemies?>>

<<I am Chu-bu,>> said one gingerbread man, <<and he is Sheemish.>>

<<No, not at all!>> said the other. <<I am Sheemish and he is Chu-bu!>>

<<But that's exactly what I said!>>

<<You certainly did not!>>

The pair began flailing at each other, and when their ineffectual blows landed, they left temporary dents in their doughy forms.

Sophronia got wearily up from her seat. <<If you can't help me, I must search on.>>

<<Who said we can't help you?>>

<<Well, we really can't, can we?>>

<<No, but we can take her to someone who can! Another creature from the Yith world. A clever ex-pat!>>

<<Must I remind you that the Yith no longer rule that planet? Why do you insist?>>

<<Oh, botheration! What's a hundred and fifty million years one way or the other? Just ignore the perversity of Chu-bu – or is he Sheemish? – O Thing from Yith, and follow us!>>

Having no other recourse, Soph lifted her leaden feet one after the other in pursuit of the pastry men.

The open door of the house where they left her cast an oblong of light onto the street. Soph stepped inside.

No fellow human occupied the front room. Only on the table stood a foot-high metal cylinder wired up to various ancillary apparatuses, featuring lenses and sounding membranes, like some kind of infernal Edison invention. Soph faltered at the unexpected sight.

<<Yes,>> said the cylinder, <<what can I do for you?>>

<<Are you a human inside such a small can?>>

<<Just my preserved brain, actually. But once I was like you, a man named Henry Akeley, from Earth. Townshend, Vermont, to be precise.>>

<<Oh, Mister Akeley, I need your help so badly!>>

Sophronia explained her twin quests. The cylinder – Akeley – was silent for a time.

<<I believe I can easily direct you to your brother. But the other matter is less clear and of more consequence. Allow me a few minutes to communicate with the Outer Beings. They are friends to humanity, and should respond helpfully.>>

Sophronia shifted from foot to foot during the interminable period of silence. She wished for a chair, but there were none. After all, what use could a brain in a tin can have for a chair? Soph's thoughts began to whirl, as she envisioned a naked brain with legs and arms and face, sitting on a stool inside its can.

<<The Outer Beings have answered. They are perturbed. Apparently, your Starry Sodality is recruiting colonists for other planets, spheres where by treaty they are not allowed. But Blank and Zhaum believe that if they can only establish a sizable presence on these worlds, they will present a *fait accompli* to rival claimants that will allow the Sodality *de facto* permanent possession of the disputed territories, and all the riches that entails. But they need many humans, not just the few disciples they have managed so far to attract. And so they intend to open up a gate and pull through hundreds of folks, willy-nilly.>>

<<They can create a rift like the one that brought me here?>>

<<Yes, but much larger, and irresistible in its gravitation.>>

Sophronia thought a moment. Where would they open up such a portal? Not on the farm in Scituate. Not even in the Amateur Dramatic Hall. Where and when might they have access to the large crowd they needed?

The Trades Procession! The Sodality float in the barn!

<<I need to find my brother and return to Earth! The Sodality must be stopped!>>

<<The Outer Beings would be glad of that. Unfortunately, they are banned from interfering directly in your affairs. They *could* send you a spell to force the gate closed. But that is, only if you had the proper instrument to receive it. I doubt you do, though, for it's a very rare item. It's called the Shining Trapezohedron...>>

<<But we do have it, we do!>>

<<Ah, that gives us a chance. I will let the Outer Beings know this, and they will download the code into the Trapezohedron's RAM.>>

Soph made no sense of this gibberish, but expressed her gratitude heartily.

<<Now, Mister Akeley, if you could just help me find my brother!>>

<<I think you will discover that he is currently the feature attraction at a place known as the Ball of Yarn. Leaving my house, turn left, then your first right, then left again, and you should find it easily. Farewell, and good luck!>>

Sophronia raced off, all weariness forgotten.

The Ball of Yarn was a tavern catering just to cats. Sophronia could smell its fishy bill of fare from a block away. She bulled in past a half dozen furry feline forms in the antechambers, and found herself in the tavern's large main room.

There on a small stage was Oscar. He was naked, save for a collar with a bell on it, and by command of a feline ringmaster cracking a whip, he was being made to jump through hoops, mount platforms and leap off, and perform other circus tricks.

Sophronia cast about wildly for some means of distraction. Her eye fell on the tavern's bar.

They did not serve liquor, but catnip, a score of different types and grades, all neatly stored in large glass jars, as on a pharmacy's shelves.

Sophronia grabbed a broom from a kitty maid, and leaped atop the wooden bar. She smashed every jar within reach.

The released flood of intoxicating leaf drove the crowd mad! They dove for the spillage, rolling in it and fighting each other, hissing, clawing, with tails inflating like bottle-brushes.

Soph jumped down, darted onstage, grabbed a dazed Oscar by the hand, and fled.

The rift home! She had not asked Akeley where it was. Now she had got turned around, and could not find his house again. She would have to pray the portal had not drifted yet from where it had deposited her. Perhaps indeed it was only the Earth-anchored end of the tunnel that drifted, for it always led to Ulthar.

On the edge of town, orienting herself by the unique configuration of the Skai River, she found the hill where she had arrived – or so she hoped. Faint tracks in the grass – cat feet and human shoes – seemed to mark the earlier passage of Clutterbuck and herself.

She sped up the hill to where the tracks ended, and flung herself and Oscar into space.

Daylight hurt her eyes, and she had to squint. When she could see, she found herself in a familiar locale. In the mouth of the alley that ran alongside Gladding's Department Store.

The sidewalk was packed with an endless sea of happy eager people. Music played from several marching bands.

Sophronia grabbed the arm of a mother busily herding five peppermint-stick-sucking children out of danger in the street.

"What's going on? What day is this?"

Before replying, the woman regarded the naked and be-collared Oscar with a rueful expression that said, *Dearie, they are a handful, aren't they?*

"Why, it's June the twenty-third, my sweets, and the big Trades Procession is about to begin!"

TEN
THE TRADES PROCESSION TO THE STARS

Several songs had been specifically commissioned for this epic occasion, receiving preview presentations at various concerts in advance of the big day, and Soph now recognised the one emitted by the passing military band as "City of Freedom".

City of beauty, favoured of God and exalted in name,
Foremost and fearless in patriotic duty, wearing her scars and
escutcheons of fame,
Struggling alone with the tempest and gloom...

She chose to regard this allusion to her patronym as a good omen.

She was exhausted and dazed, her head filled with strange new wonders. She was saddled with a naked little brother, deprived of a couple of weeks of her mortal existence whilst under Elf Hill, and utterly famished. She had no idea of what her parents or her friends thought of her long inexplicable absence. Maybe they considered her dead, and had already finished mourning her. She had no immediate notion of how best to contact Professor Charnley and inform him of the exact nature of Blank & Zhaum's plot, along with apprising him of the new potency instilled in the Shining Trapezohedron by the Outer Beings in order to counter those schemes. But despite all these burdens and obstacles, she felt imbued with hope and courage and a sense of possible victory. Look at what she had already endured. There was no chance in Hades that she would let the Starry Sodality pillage her city!

But first things first.

Sophronia again addressed, with some urgency, the friendly woman with her unruly brood, who stood now in her eyes as a symbol of all the goodness she was striving to protect.

"Please, ma'am, what is your name? I am Sophronia Tempest. My father is Clarence Tempest, vice-president at Kendall Manufacturing Company."

"Why, they make Soapine! 'Soapine, the Dirt Killer! It Washes Everything!' I couldn't manage my household without it! Oh, yes, I'm Clara Spink. And my children – stop that! – are Gustavus, Billy, Lucy, Wendell and Linnie."

"Clara, I must impinge upon your charity with several requests. First, tell me the hour, and exactly when the Procession commences."

"Why, it's ten AM, and the first wagons do not roll until eleven. My husband is Barton Spink, you know, of Murray, Spink and Company, Fancy Goods. They have four drays in the Procession. One features a giant cigar, one displays Tally-Ho shirts, one shows glassware in a pyramid, and the last portrays a giant American Eagle. The children can't wait to see their father pass by and cheer him on."

Gustavus – or was that Wendell? – crossed his eyes and stuck out his tongue.

An hour till the Procession took off. Surely the Starry Sodality would wait to trigger the cosmic gate until their wagon reached the place on the route with the largest concentration of people. Not the beginning, nor the end. But where would that be?

The Mayoral Reviewing Stand, planned to have been erected at the intersection of Sutton and Broadway, not far from Soph's home!

Soph returned her attention to Clara Spink, who was casting a bemused glance at this young, wild-eyed woman accompanied by a nude boy. Sophronia could only imagine what the matron was thinking.

"Clara, I must ask you to please take charge of my little brother, Oscar. I cannot send him home, for my parents are no doubt off the premises, busy with this very Procession. Nor can I take him with me, for I am about to embark on a dangerous errand. Would you do me this immense favour?"

"Why, certainly! What's one more child when you've got five? Oscar, come over here, dear."

From a capacious carpetbag, Clara Spink removed a fresh shirt.

"Billy is always spilling things on himself, so I came prepared."

She dressed Oscar in the overlarge garment that served to cover his indecency, and handed him a peppermint stick.

"Might I have one of those too, Clara? I very much need a boost."

Soph instantly bit off half the proffered candy and crunched it. It tasted heavenly.

She crouched down to Oscar's level, and removed the Ulthar collar from his neck. Inert till now, the boy seemed to be gradually regaining his normal demeanour and feisty spirit.

"Oscar, you stay with Mrs. Spink for now. If I don't return for you, just go to our home at the end of the day."

Assuming there's a house to return to, she mentally added.

"All right, Soph."

Sophronia made ready to leave, for she now had a destination in mind.

"Soph?"

"Yes?"

"You won't never tell no one about – about me on stage with the cats, will you?"

"No, never! That will be our little secret."

Clara Spink was wiping Lucy's nose – or was that Linnie's? – when Soph made her grateful adieu.

Then, rucking up her skirts, she began to run – to run as she never had, even on the playing fields of St. Mary's!

Gladding's Department Store was midtown. Brown University's New Library was many blocks away, and some of those blocks uphill at that.

Even weaving through the crowds and having to wait for gaps in the festive marchers in order to cross certain streets, Sophronia made remarkable time. Nonetheless, she felt extremely ragged and could barely draw a breath when she reached the corner of Prospect and Waterman.

There, much to her surprise, she saw the *Journal* carriage parked out front! Pausing just a moment to recover herself, she laid a hand briefly on the nose of the loyal, night-gaunt-tested bay stallion, then dashed up the library steps.

One flight, two flights, three flights, then the ladder!

Halfway emergent through the trap door and into the Professor's eyrie, Soph paused.

The tiny room was stuffed with her friends: the Professor, Crispus Bannister, Mack Callender – and Reuben Standeven.

Grinning broadly, this last-named now said, "Murderin' Irishman, my girl! What took you so long?"

In order to reach Broadway and Sutton, the *Journal* carriage could not take the shortest, most direct route, east to west, for all the intervening streets were filled with marchers and spectators. They had to detour by Smith Hill, making a big loop around the congested downtown. The Trades Procession would begin from Market Square and thread its way down Westminster and Jackson streets before reaching the reviewing stand on Broadway. This slow and prolonged course for the exhibitors, combined with Crispus Bannister's expert driving and navigation, should afford them enough time to beat the first display wagon there.

And, giving additional insurance, the Starry Sodality entry, a latecomer to the ranks, would be the final dray, preceding only a smattering of lesser tradesmen who followed in simple fashion, merely astride their horses or on foot.

Sophronia sat beside the Professor. In his lap rested the elaborate chest that contained the Shining Trapezohedron. Additionally, the Professor's person was encumbered with a dozen other enigmatic and esoteric charms, pinned to his vest or strung on cords around his neck. In one case, they featured as a large silver cuff studded with several gems. His normally relaxed and ruminative visage was tautened with an undeniable tension kept under firm control.

Across the way sat Reuben and Callender. Soph felt gratitude towards her boss for throwing in his lot with their ragtag bunch. But she still nursed some shreds of vexation for her co-worker. He had greeted her reappearance so blithely, and with such frivolity, that she could hardly credit him with any tender or noble feelings. This was not the way a girl liked to be received when she returned from the dead!

What a head-spinning interval she had just endured!

When Soph had recovered her wits and clambered fully into the cupola, she had been greeted with joy and warmth by the other three men. And, truth be told, even Reuben had moderated his innate flippancy to make her feel that her homecoming was special. And in short order, wasting none of their precious time, the Professor had explained to her how and why they had been awaiting her.

"You recall that on the day Oscar disappeared I left you in order to employ my scrying stone? Well, sure enough, after some long hours of finessing, I was able to pick up visual traces of his passage to Ulthar. And while I was trying to design the best way to convince your parents of his occult whereabouts, you showed up in the stone's purview as well!"

Reuben chimed in. "We watched your every action there! Crikey, you moved slow as molasses. We could step away for hours, and you barely shifted your pinky finger."

"Yes," affirmed Charnley, "the temporal disparities between the two continua were enormous."

Reuben said, "We couldn't *hear* a blessed thing, of course, with that damn silly stone, but over time we saw it all. That was a treble-ex job you did rescuing your brother!"

"Please, don't ever reveal you witnessed his humiliation!"

"Oh, we shan't," said the Professor. "But in any case, I was finally able to use the stone to convince your parents that you were both somewhat safe. Well, not precisely safe, but at least accounted for, and with a good prospect of returning home eventually."

"So they don't think Oscar and I are dead?"

"Oh my, no. They finally accepted your spatial displacement from the fields we know, and understood the need for secrecy. To calm the searchers, they put out the story that a relative had taken Oscar to Boston in a confusion of arrangements, and that you had gone there too, for a vacation. They are still anxious for your return, of course. When, several days ago, we saw you start to run up the hill in Ulthar and toward the rift, we calculated exactly when you would pop back out in Providence."

"But not where, of course," Reuben added. "Which is why you had no welcoming committee."

"We had to assume you'd have the wits to search me out here. And so we just waited."

Sophronia hastily assimilated all this information about her missing weeks. She was glad to have this confirmation of her incredible experiences. And she felt a little proud at the compliments paid her initiative and boldness. But with a sudden shock, she realised that the clock was still ticking toward the moment when Blank & Zhaum would initiate their catastrophe.

"Professor, I must tell you what I learned from Mister Akeley, that disembodied brain! It's a most perfidious scheme!"

"Ah," exclaimed Reuben, "we wondered why you were fussing so long with that old jam jar!"

Professor Charnley and the others listened keenly to Sophronia's account. When she had finished, silence obtained, until the Professor spoke their mutual thoughts.

"This is worse than I could have imagined. A gigantic crack in space that will siphon off our citizens… But you came back with a weapon."

He excused himself to retrieve the Shining Trapezohedron and test its new capacities.

Soph turned to her editor. "Mister Callender, I am most heartened to find you here. But how did you get involved?"

"Why, your partner in crime, Mister Standeven, saw fit to enrol me. He explained everything you had discovered about the Starry Sodality, and how you two were on the point of breaking the biggest story this town had ever seen. But more crucially, when I learned that these bastards planned to harm our fair city in some diabolical fashion, I knew I had to play a part in foiling them."

Reuben added, "I wish we could have convinced other powers that be to join in as well. But the Mayor, the police, the Governor, major businessmen, firemen, the militias, the Grange – no one would listen to us. They all said we were barmy. Actually, I think some of them were in league with Blank and company. Oh, not that they knew about her ultimate scheme, but they had been won over to her airy-fairy pipe dreams. Her personal charm was considerable, as we can attest."

"So it's just we five against them?"

Professor Charnley had finished putting the talisman through its new paces. He took the time to demonstrate for Sophronia the simple sigils which activated the device, making sure she had them pat, even guiding her hand in the patterns until the gestures became a bodily memory. Then he addressed her concern.

"Yes, it's all up to us. But we five should suffice. Our defence must of necessity be a simple one that does not require a large force. Here is what I envision. Blank and Zhaum open the gate, leading to a world of their choosing. They hope to pull through scores, if not hundreds of our fellows, and then, I believe, to follow them, leaving behind our depredated globe for their intended destination. But the instant they activate the flaw in space, I will change its attunement to a far less salubrious destination, using the Trapezohedron's new powers. We shove our two malefactors through, and then I close the whole shebang down. They shall never be able to return."

"But," reasoned Sophronia, "won't we lose at least a few innocent bystanders into the sucking void while all this is going on?"

Charnley looked grim. "I fear it will be unavoidable. Which is why we must move as fast as possible when the time comes. Now, as to the possible location of our defence –"

Sophronia jumped in with her logic about the reviewing stand, and found quick concord from the others. And so they hastened off.

Now in the cab of the carriage, Sophronia ceased her musings when the Professor tapped her on the arm with a small envelope.

"Miss Tempest, I'd like you to hold onto this letter for me. If all goes well, I shall reclaim it. If I suffer a misadventure, then you may read it."

"But Professor, you won't –"

"Shush! Just do as I ask, please."

Having lost her reticule somewhere in Ulthar, Soph had no recourse but to lift her skirt and tuck the folded envelope into the top of her high shoe. Callender and Charnley averted their eyes at the display, but Reuben stared and then whistled!

That boy was the absolute worst!

After making their wide circumambulation, Crispus brought them efficiently to the block of Sutton Street on Federal Hill, parallel to Broadway. They followed the cross street as far as they could before the crowds near the Broadway intersection halted their progress. They jumped out and hurried the last distance on foot.

On Broadway, they encountered the grand reviewing stand from the rear, all tricked out in colourful bunting. The platform was filled with frock-coated, top-hatted gents and their ladies in finery and ostrich-feather-plumed chapeaus. Bulling their way to the front ranks of the numerous spectators, the quintet arrived at curbside just as one of the many dignitaries – Chief Justice Durfee, in fact – was launching into a speech.

"The traveller who, after a long day's journey, reaches the summit of some high hill which overlooks the way behind him, delights to pause with backward gaze and review the scenes through which he has passed. His memory fills out the picture; until at last his whole journey, tedious sometimes in the making, lies before him, flooded with the golden evening light, a pure and perfect pleasure in the retrospect. Today the city pauses on such a high spectacular summit, and, looking backward through the vista of two hundred and fifty years, sees the long series of her historic experiences rising in visionary pageant before her..."

Within minutes of Durfee's tedious conclusion, the first float rolled up: Branden & Keep, Flour Merchants.

Sophronia at first felt a vast impatience and worry, and she shifted nervously from foot to foot, eyeing her fellow defenders with anxious imploring glances.

But then, as more and more floats came by, under the glorious June sun and to the cheers of the spectators, a curious phenomenon overtook her. The array of familiar products and plain faces, the evident exultancy and pride of the marchers, the excitement and joy of the crowd – everything conspired to instil in her a kind of placid confidence, a homely assurance that evil could not prevail against this bulwark of honest commerce, exemplary of mankind's desire to make a better world.

When the float from Murray, Spink and Company, Fancy Goods, passed, she grinned to imagine the excitement of Mrs Spink and her flock, with Oscar there too.

And when the Soapine float came by, displaying a giant whale being scrubbed by a team of Esquimaux, and she saw her father and mother smiling and waving proudly aloft, she reached a zenith of transcendent calm.

And greatly would she need all her inner resources, for finally the Starry Sodality dray was approaching! Its contorted alien jungle scene, painted in eye-jarring colours, loomed even more hideously by light of day than it had in the Scituate barn. At the rear of the wagon bed stood the immodestly alluring Isadora Blank and the uncannily repugnant Knygathin Zhaum.

And their perverted diorama was rendered even more obscene by the placement of the unsuspecting robed acolytes among the fake vegetation.

Soph saw Arthur, standing like a pompous fool. She wanted to call out a warning to him, but dared not alert Blank and Zhaum, so she bit her tongue. Would he even have responded? She was never to know.

As no other dray had done, the Sodality float came to a halt in front of the reviewing stand, causing at first mild consternation from the dignitaries and from the marchers behind, who also bumbled to a forced stop.

Isadora Blank could not resist making a taunting speech. Focused entirely on the important people, she was paying no attention to the rabble at her feet. This distraction allowed Crispus, Reuben and Callender to scuttle out into the street and merge with the marchers at the rear of the wagon, a company of lumbermen and foresters, all arrayed in their best gear. Soph remained next to the Professor, to assist as she might.

"Witless cattle!" bellowed the Hierophant. "You will now serve your only true purpose in life. To glorify the Elder Gods!"

With this, she began to chant those incomprehensible syllables, or their kin, that Soph had first heard at the lecture hall, seemingly undead eons ago.

On a plane in the air between and slightly to the forward of Blank and Zhaum, a shimmery opalescent curtain began to form. Within seconds, it had transformed to an impossible window, opening onto the alien world that had served as the model for the float! The air of Providence began to move, pulled into the portal. At first the flow was mild, just enough to snatch all the hats from the dignitaries. But soon, within seconds, it began to increase in speed and power.

The closest acolytes were snatched off their feet and sucked through the well of worlds, wailing! The other dupes began to shriek and clutch at the jungle display. But soon they too were pulled in, along with the debris.

With utter horror, Sophronia witnessed Arthur being whipped off his feet, flying away forever, to a place where no elegant crockery prevailed.

Members of the audience and the dignitaries on the stand began to feel the increasing power of the opened interstellar door. They clutched at the more secure railings or at lamp posts or each other, and for a while could resist. But as the vortex increased by the second, they would soon succumb. And who knew how strong the winds would become, how many square blocks would be devastated?

Standing to the rear of the portal and its unidirectional suction, Zhaum and Blank were safe, laughing and urging on the chaos.

Professor Charnley's fingers were inscribing those patterns he had shown Soph on the surface of the Trapezohedron.

"Now!" he shouted.

Everything seemed to happen simultaneously.

The vista in the portal changed to a roiling, burbling hellscape full of a thousand demonic yellow eyes, the intended doom for Blank and Zhaum – and, unfortunately, for anyone else who might yet be plucked.

Reuben and the one-armed Mack Callender jumped up alongside the startled Zhaum. Callender dropped to his knees and a single hand in front of the tall spidery fellow, and Reuben slammed into Zhaum from behind. The combined child-like gamefield manoeuvre thrust the giant off his feet and into the maelstrom of wind. He was instantly sucked, gibbering and flailing his boneless limbs, into the churning pool of balefire, along with one or two innocents from the shrieking crowd who had lost their holds.

Crispus was struggling with Isadora. But the supposedly easy task of shoving the lightweight woman off her feet proved surprisingly hard.

For Isadora Blank now revealed her true form.

She had devolved into a writhing mass of ivory protoplasm, all human semblance lost in a nest of whipping tendrils, clattering beaks, stalked eyeballs, and suckered pseudopods, which poked through her ripped robe.

Crispus battled the snaky appendages mightily, but to no seeming avail. Enwrapped around the waist, he was losing ground fast, and faced being hurled into the vortex.

Sophronia raced out into the street, grabbed a lumberman's axe from his slack hands, and heaved it up to the valiant Negro.

With several bold strokes he freed himself, although without appearing to inflict mortal harm on his assailant.

And the momentarily balked thing that had been Isadora Blank was no closer to the portal than before.

Sophronia found something thrust into her hands.

The Shining Trapezohedron!

"Do as I showed you!" yelled Professor Charnley. "Don't hesitate, no matter what! And do not fear! Not now, nor ever!"

For a plump, older fellow, the Professor could move adroitly. He got aboard the dray, hooking one leg and an arm around a stanchion that threatened to splinter. He ripped one of the charms from around his neck and flourished it where Isadora could see it with her multiple eyes.

It must have been a potent treasure indeed, perhaps even enough to save the day for evil. She cast forward a tentacle to snatch it.

Charnley grabbed the tentacle with both hands, released his leg hold, and cast himself into the suction, his mass serving to pull Isadora off her base and carry her with him.

Soph witnessed a look of fulfilled serenity on the savant's face before he vanished.

Almost of their own accord, her fingers danced across the reactive surface of the Shining Trapezohedron.

The portal closed down instantly, as if it had never been.

Weeping and lamentations and groans resounded, along with the creaking of wooden structures released from the devil wind's grip.

Only when Reuben had taken her in his arms did Sophronia realise that some of the tears were hers.

Bertha, flushed and smiling proudly, had outdone herself, with nary a culinary misstep. The feast spread out at 380 Broadway for the Fourth of July would have sufficed for a crowd of twenty. Platters were heaped with meats and vegetables and salads, rolls, pickles and olives, while puddings and sweets brought up the rear. Sparkling wine filled every glass.

But the attendees at the victory celebration and commemoration of the nation's birth were only seven in number: the four Tempests; Mack Callender; Crispus Bannister; and Reuben Standeven.

An eighth place, never to be occupied, had been set for Professor Charnley, and adorned with a wreath.

Outside in the street, cheers and the snap of firecrackers resounded.

Sophronia gazed around the table lovingly. Here were all those most dear to her, those who had gone through hell with her to preserve their fair city, and to be here today, safe and sound.

She even included in those ranks that utter unrepentant jackanapes, Reuben Standeven, whose engagement ring now graced her finger. A paltry gem, consonant with a reporter's salary, but magnificent in her eyes.

After all the toasts had been made, and at least a partial justice paid to the food, and after Minnie Tempest had updated her list of wedding guests with some afterthoughts about distant relatives, Mack Callender said, "Well, Miss Tempest, I do not suppose that you will be returning to your desk at the *Journal*, now that you have a marriage in your future."

"I shall not be. But it is no vow of wedlock that dissuades me from that. Instead, it is my legacy from the Professor."

Only when wearily undressing on the night of the Trades Procession disaster had Soph come upon the unremembered envelope saved in her shoe. Its contents had consisted of Professor Charnley's last will and testament, in which he bequeathed all his vast library and collections to Sophronia Tempest, to employ as she saw fit.

Before Callender could speak further, Oscar suddenly gave a yelp.

"Papa, this bad cat scratched me!"

The family's new pet – a calico named Tuppence, who had appeared from nowhere one day to attach herself to the family – sauntered out from underneath the table, wearing a particularly *knowing* look.

"Well," said Clarence Tempest, "I'm sure you were at fault in teasing her. Need I mention a certain tavern to you?"

Oscar paled, and hunched down in his seat. "No, Papa. I'll be good!"

Callender resumed the thread of his conversation. "So, Miss Tempest, you intend to pick up where Professor Charnley left off? Protecting our city from any future occult harm?"

"Yes, that is my goal. But do not use the word 'occult', I pray you. After all, it's merely science of a different sort, in line with what I've always pursued. There's positively no magic involved."

Reuben's laughter belled out. "Why, my darling scamp, you are stuffed so full of blessed magic that it's leaking out your gorgeous little fingers!"

He took her hand in his. The stone in her ring was all aflame.

ABOUT THE AUTHOR

Paul Di Filippo has published over forty books, with his newest novel being *The Summer Thieves*, a Vancian space opera. He lives in Providence, RI, with his partner Deborah Newton and a cocker spaniel named Moxie.

Also from NewCon Press

Steampunk International edited by Ian Whates
English language edition of an anthology showcasing the very best Steampunk stories from three different countries: UK, Finland, and Italy; released by three different publishers in three different languages. UK contributors are George Mann (an original Newbury and Hobbes tale), Jonathan Green, Derry O'Dowd.

Best of British SF 2021 edited by Donna Scott
Two dozen of the best stories written by British and British-based authors during 2021, as selected by series editor Donna Scott. Features stories by Paul Cornell, Liz Williams, Keith Brooke and Eric Brown, Aliya Whiteley, Fiona Moore, Nick Wood, Martin Sketchley, and more.

The Double-Edged Sword – Ian Whates
Fleeing a backwater town one step ahead of the law and tiring of his dubious life style, the Fallen Hero seeks employment in the port of Cray. But his past catches up with him and he is forced to embark on what looks to be a suicide mission… unless he can beat the odds.

Night, Rain, and Neon edited by Michael Cobley
All new cyberpunk stories from Ian McDonald, Louise Carey, Jon Courtenay Grimwood, Justina Robson, Simon Morden, Gary Gibson, DA Xiaolin Spires, Al Robertson, Keith Brooke & Eric Brown, T.R. Napper, Jeremy Szal, Gavin Smith, Tim Maughan, Stewart Hotston and more.

The Wild Hunt – Garry Kilworth
When Gods meddle in the affairs of mortals, it never ends well… for the mortals, at any rate. An epic Anglo-Saxon saga featuring warriors, witches, giants, dwarfs, light elves and more, set during the Darker Ages before Christianity.

www.newconpress.co.uk

www.ingramcontent.com/pod-product-compliance
Lightning Source LLC
Chambersburg PA
CBHW030354180626
46812CB00007B/2880